PUFFIN BOOKS

Stories for Five-Year-Olds

...me they are five, most children are confident enough
...miliar world of home and school to want to explore
...beyond. This is a time when new experiences beckon
...n the imagination is ready to take wing: stories of
...nd suspense are delighted in. But whatever trials and
...encountered on the way, there must always be the
...expectation of the happy ending.

...ection of twenty-two stories has been specially
...these twin needs in mind by two celebrated story-
...and story-tellers, and has been tested on individual
...nd groups of five-year-olds. Here are tales to stir the
...n and yet reassure the timid. Betty, who meets a
...er way to school; a brand-new engine learning its
...ong – and a monkey divining Archimedes' principle
...help of an obliging hippopotamus!). There are
...cient and modern: old heroes (Tom Thumb) and
...ends (Bobby Brewster). All will be enjoyed by lis-
...teller alike.

...help the story-teller there is a note of encourage-
...advice to grown-ups on how to make the most of
...iest occupation – reading to children.

...orrin has made the subject of children's responses to
...one of her main studies. She is a Senior Lecturer in
...on and specializes in child development. Born within
...of Bow Bells, she has all the Cockney's good
...and jaunty repartee. Stephen Corrin, her husband,
...ght up on a mixed diet of the *Gem*, the *Magnet*, the
...cket and Beethoven quartets. He reviews, writes
...nd translates from French, Russian, German and
Da...

D1392123

Stories for Five-Year-Olds

and other young readers

EDITED BY

SARA & STEPHEN CORRIN

ILLUSTRATED BY

SHIRLEY HUGHES

Puffin Books

in association with **Faber and Faber**

PUFFIN BOOKS

Published by the Penguin Group
27 Wrights Lane, London w8 5tz, England
Viking Penguin Inc., 40 West 23rd Street, New York, New York 10010, USA
Penguin Books Australia Ltd, Ringwood, Victoria, Australia
Penguin Books Canada Ltd, 2801 John Street, Markham, Ontario, Canada l3r 1b4
Penguin Books (NZ) Ltd, 182–190 Wairau Road, Auckland 10, New Zealand

Penguin Books Ltd, Registered Offices: Harmondsworth, Middlesex, England

This collection (with five more stories) first published by Faber and Faber 1973
Published in Puffin Books 1976
21 23 25 27 29 30 28 26 24 22

Copyright © Faber and Faber Ltd, 1973
Illustrations copyright © Faber and Faber Ltd, 1973
All rights reserved

Made and printed in Great Britain by
Richard Clay Ltd, Bungay, Suffolk
Set in Linotype Baskerville

Contents

Contents

A Word to the
Story-Teller

BY the age of five or thereabouts most children have come to grips sufficiently with reality and feel secure enough in the world they know to venture forth and explore the mysterious and exciting world beyond.

But just as with their own little sorties they constantly return to base for reassurance, so in the stories they hear they are ready to grapple with suspense, trials and fears (by identification with the characters) so long as the perils are followed by a complete and wholly reassuring return to home and serenity. The final note of comfort and security is essential to satisfy a fundamental need.

The stories in this volume combine the familiar elements which a child requires with fantasy and humour. But there is none of your tame spending-a-day-at-the-launderette stuff. These tales will feed the child's sense of fun and stir his imagination. Ancient and modern, they come from all corners of the earth. Many of them are traditional but we have included a goodly sprinkling of contemporary writers.

The question, of course, must be asked: can stories be so rigidly classified as to justify the title *Stories for Five-Year-Olds*? Most teachers will say they can, which does not, however, imply that the same stories will not be of interest to other age groups. Rather it suggests that every age has differing emotional and intellectual requirements and that there are some stories very much more suited than others to meet these requirements. Each age-range – and each child within this range – will draw from the story at different levels, according to need and experience; so that in a class of thirty five-year-olds one is catering for thirty individuals. And yet the whole class will sit entranced, linked by some magic spell.

The collection has been tried out and proved its worth with classes of five-year-olds, as well as with individual children. It will help, of course, if the teacher reads them in such a way as to convey her own enthusiasm to her audience. This goes for the parent, too, as well as for the aunt or elder sister. The story-teller should not shrink from adding a little trimming here and there, for these stories are highly condensed affairs. A word or phrase may be freely adapted to suit the capacity or temperament of the listener. And above all, the teller must not fight shy of dramatizing – young people show an almost instinctive response to dramatic suspense. All this is safely within the story-telling tradition; over the many, many years that these tales have been handed down, they have been added to and embellished in all sorts of ways. But never, of course, beyond recognition. The basic themes remain: we find them appearing in various guises in all parts of the world.

A Word to the Story-Teller

Editor's note:

We have left out the following five stories from the original hardback collection, since they are already published in full in other Puffin editions.   They are:

'The Acorn Man' by Ruth Ainsworth (from *The Ten Tales of Shellover*)

'Little Old Mrs Pepperpot' by Alf Proysen

'Clever Polly and the Stupid Wolf' by Catherine Storr

'The Stamping Elephant' by Anita Hewett (from *The Anita Hewett Animal Story Book*)

'Teddy Robinson's Night Out' by Joan G. Robinson (from *About Teddy Robinson*)

Lion at School

ONCE upon a time there was a little girl who didn't like going to school. She always set off late. Then she had to hurry, but she never hurried fast enough.

One morning she was hurrying along as usual when she turned a corner and there stood a lion, blocking her way. He stood waiting for her. He stared at her with his yellow eyes. He growled, and when he growled the little girl could see that his teeth were as sharp as skewers and knives. He growled: 'I'm going to eat you up.'

'Oh, dear!' said the little girl, and she began to cry.

'Wait!' said the lion. 'I haven't finished. I'm going to eat you up UNLESS you take me to school with you.'

'Oh, dear!' said the little girl. 'I couldn't do that. My teacher says we mustn't bring pets to school.'

'I'm not a pet,' said the lion. He growled again, and she saw that his tail swished from side to side in anger – *swish! swash! swish! swash!* 'You can tell your teacher that I'm a friend who is coming to school with you,' he said. 'Now shall we go?'

The little girl had stopped crying. She said: 'All right. But you must promise two things. First of all, you mustn't eat anyone: it's not allowed.'

'I suppose I can growl?' said the lion.

'I suppose you can,' said the little girl.

'And I suppose I can roar?'

'Must you?' said the little girl.

'Yes,' said the lion.

'Then I suppose you can,' said the little girl.

'And what's the second thing?' asked the lion.

'You must let me ride on your back to school.'

'Very well,' said the lion.

He crouched down on the pavement and the little girl climbed on his back. She held on by his mane. Then they went on together towards the school, the little girl riding the lion.

The lion ran with the little girl on his back to school. Even so, they were late. The little girl and the lion went into the classroom just as the teacher was calling the register.

The teacher stopped calling the register when she saw the little girl and the lion. She stared at the lion, and all the other children stared at the lion, wondering what the teacher was going to say. The teacher said to the little girl: 'You know you are not allowed to bring pets to school.'

The lion began to swish his tail – *swish! swash!* The little girl said quickly: 'This is not a pet. This is my friend who is coming to school with me.'

The teacher still stared at the lion, but she said to the little girl: 'What is his name then?'

'Noil,' said the little girl. 'His name is Noil. Just Noil.' She knew it would be no good to tell the teacher that her friend was a lion, so she had turned his name backwards: LION – NOIL.

The teacher wrote the name down in the register: NOIL. Then she finished calling the register.

'Betty Small,' she said.

'Yes,' said the little girl.

'Noil,' said the teacher.

'Yes,' said the lion. He mumbled, opening his mouth as little as possible, so that the teacher should not see his teeth as sharp as skewers and knives. He did not swish

his tail. He did not growl. He sat next to the little girl as good as gold.

All that morning the lion sat up on his chair next to the little girl, like a big cat, with his tail curled round his front paws, as good as gold. No one saw his teeth, no one saw his claws. He didn't speak unless the teacher spoke to him. He didn't growl, he didn't roar.

At playtime the little girl showed the lion how to drink milk through a straw.

'This is milk,' she said. 'It makes your teeth grow strong.'

'Good,' said the lion. 'I want my teeth to be strong to crunch bones.'

He finished his milk up.

They went into the playground. All the children stopped playing to stare at the lion. Then they went on playing again. The little girl stood in a corner of the playground, with the lion beside her.

'Why don't we play like the others?' the lion asked.

The little girl said, 'I don't like playing because some of the big boys are so big and rough. They knock you over without meaning to.'

The lion growled. 'They wouldn't knock ME over,' he said.

'There's one big boy – the very biggest,' said the little girl. 'His name is Jack Tall. He knocks me over on purpose.'

'Which is he?' said the lion. 'Point him out to me.'

The little girl pointed out Jack Tall to the lion.

'Ah!' said the lion. 'So that's Jack Tall.'

Just then the bell rang again, and all the children went back to their classrooms. The lion went with the little girl and sat beside her while the teacher read a story aloud.

Then the children drew and wrote until dinnertime. The lion was hungry, so he wanted to draw a picture of his dinner.

'What will it be for dinner?' he asked the little girl. 'I hope it's meat.'

'No,' said the little girl. 'It will be fish fingers because today is Friday.'

Then the little girl showed the lion how to hold the

yellow crayon in his paw and draw fish fingers. Underneath his picture she wrote: 'I like meat better than fish fingers.'

Then it was dinnertime. The lion sat up on his chair at the dinner-table next to the little girl. There were fish fingers for dinner, with peas and mashed potatoes. Afterwards there was cake and custard. The lion ate everything on his plate, and then he ate anything that the little girl had left on her plate. He ate very fast and at the end he said: 'I'm still hungry; and I wish it had been meat.'

After dinner all the children went into the playground.

All the big boys were running about, and the very biggest boy, Jack Tall, came running towards the little girl. He was running in circles, closer and closer to the little girl.

'Go away,' said the lion. 'You might knock my friend over. Go away.'

'Shan't,' said Jack Tall. The little girl got behind the lion.

The lion began to swish his tail: *swish! swash!*

Jack Tall was running closer and closer and closer.

The lion growled. Then Jack Tall saw the lion's teeth as sharp as skewers and knives. He stopped running. He stood still. He stared.

The lion opened his mouth wider – so wide that Jack Tall could see his throat, opened wide and deep and dark like a tunnel to go into. Jack Tall went pale.

Then the lion roared.

He roared and he ROARED and he ROARED.

All the teachers came running out, to see what the matter was.

All the children stopped playing and stuck their fingers in their ears. And the biggest boy, Jack Tall, turned round and ran and ran and ran – out of the playground – out through the school gates – along the

streets. He never stopped running until he got home to his mother.

The little girl came out from behind the lion. 'Well,' she said, 'I don't think much of *him*. I shall never be scared of *him* again.'

'I was hungry,' said the lion, 'I could easily have eaten him. Only I'd promised you.'

'And his mother wouldn't have liked it,' said the little girl. 'Time for afternoon school now.'

'I'm not staying for afternoon school,' said the lion.

'See you on Monday then,' said the little girl. But the lion did not answer. He just walked off.

On Monday morning the little girl started in good time for school, because she was looking forward to it. She arrived in good time, too.

She did not see the lion.

In the classroom the teacher called the register.

She came to the little girl's name.

'Betty Small,' she said.

'Yes,' said the little girl.

'Noil,' said the teacher.

No one answered.

Later on, in the playground, the biggest boy came up to the little girl.

'Where's your friend that talks so loudly?' he said.

'He's not here today,' said the little girl.

'Might he come another day?' asked the biggest boy.

'He might,' said the little girl. 'He easily might. So you just watch out, Jack Tall.'

One Little Pig
and Ten Wolves

ONCE upon a time a little pig lived in a little wooden shack in the middle of a forest in Hungary. He looked after himself very well, sweeping his house clean every morning, fetching fresh water from the stream and collecting twigs and small branches which had fallen from the tall forest trees, for his fire.

One very cold day when the north wind was blowing and snow was in the air, the little pig kindled a bigger fire than usual in the fireplace of his little house, and began cooking his dinner.

Suddenly he heard a banging on his door, and a voice which the little pig recognized at once as that of a wolf, shouted:

'*Dear little pig! Kind little pig! Do let me in.*'

'Dear little pig! Kind little pig! Do let me in. The north wind is blowing and I am freezing to death.'

'Certainly not!' exclaimed the little pig. 'If I let you in here, you will eat me.'

'Of course I won't eat you!' said the wolf. 'But if you would open the door and let me put just one of my back legs into the warmth of your house, that would save me from dying of cold.'

Now the little pig knew from experience how wretched it was to be cold, and since he had a kind heart, and thought that one back leg of the wolf could not do him any harm, he replied, 'Very well. Only one back leg and no more.'

'Thank you! Thank you! Dear little pig, kind little pig,' said the wolf in what he hoped was a gentle voice.

So the little pig opened the door just wide enough

for the wolf to put in one back leg, but as he did not really trust the wolf, he decided to keep a wary eye on him.

All was quiet for some time until with a deep sigh the wolf said, 'Dear little pig! Kind little pig! Will you let me put my other back leg in your house? The north wind is still blowing and I am so cold. Just one more leg is all I ask of you.'

So the kind little pig let the wolf bring in his other

back leg, and lie down with half his body inside and half outside.

The little pig busied himself stoking up his fire and the wolf appeared to go to sleep, but presently he began sighing loudly and said, 'Dear little pig! Kind little pig! You can see that I have no intention of harming you. Please let me bring in my front legs, for they are frozen stiff with the cold. I will leave my head outside, but do please let me bring in my front legs.'

'All right,' said the little pig, 'but you must promise not to harm me.'

So the wolf moved backwards until the whole of his body was inside the house, and the little pig put even more wood on the fire.

Presently the wolf began sighing and grunting again, and exclaimed:

'Dear little pig! Kind little pig! You cannot imagine what it is like for me to keep my head out here in the cold. There is ice round my mouth and nose and I can scarcely breathe. Do let the rest of me in, and I will promise not to harm you.'

Now there was a large sack and a piece of thick string on the floor of the little pig's house, and before answering he picked these up. Then carefully holding the sack open behind the wolf the little pig said, 'Very well. But come in backwards very carefully so that you do not break my door down.'

So the wolf wriggled carefully backwards until his whole body was inside the house. But what he did not realize until it was too late, was that his whole body was now inside the sack.

Quick as a flash, the little pig tied up the mouth of the sack with string; then rushing outside he called to his friends the bees, who were taking their winter sleep in a nearby hollow tree.

'Bees! Bees!' he cried. 'Wake up and come and help me! The bad wolf has pushed his way into my house, and I know he means to eat me.'

Almost at once a swarm of angry, buzzing bees flew towards the little pig, and when he pointed to the wriggling sack, they all knew what to do. One by one they squeezed through the tiny gap where the pig had tied the string, and they began to sting the wolf all over his body.

The wolf threw himself about inside the sack with such vigour, that after a while the top burst open and he started to crawl out.

When the little pig saw this happening, he ran round to the back of his house where there was a ladder leaning against the wall. Up he climbed, and then with a mighty heave, pulled the ladder on to the roof beside him and hid behind the chimney pot.

Meanwhile the wolf had rushed off to fetch some of his bad friends, for he was determined to get even with the little pig.

When they could not find him, they began looking up in the trees and on the roof until, at last, one of them caught sight of the little pig crouching behind the chimney.

'There he is!' shouted the wolf, and all ten wolves stood staring at the roof, discussing how they could get at the little pig.

As there was no ladder for the wolves to climb, the little pig thought he was quite safe, but when he realized what they were planning, he was horrified.

'I will stand here,' said the first wolf who had been tied up in the sack, 'and one of you must climb on to my back. Then the others must get up one by one, until we have made a wolf-ladder, and then we shall be able to reach the little pig.'

So the first wolf stood close to the wall of the house, while the others began to climb up on to each other's backs, higher and higher, getting closer and closer to the little pig.

But just as the tenth wolf was clambering over all the other wolves to get to the top, the little pig shouted:

'Bees! Bees! Come back and help me! The bad wolf is after me again.'

The first wolf, who was still smarting from the pain of being stung so badly, was terrified, and without thinking of the consequences he dashed away from the house as fast as he could go, causing the nine other wolves to crash down on the ground in a struggling heap.

Some of them fell so heavily that they broke their necks and died, and the others ran away as fast as they could into the forest, and never came back.

When the little pig was sure he was safe, he lowered the ladder, climbed down, and went back into his little house, bolting the door firmly.

Never again was he troubled by wolves, and certainly never by the bad wolf, who went away and hid himself until the bee stings had stopped hurting, and then decided to go and live in a different part of the forest, as far away from the little pig's house as he could go.

Tim Rabbit's Magic Cloak

It was autumn, the beech leaves were falling from the great trees and covering the ground with a carpet of russet brown. Tim Rabbit came hurrying out of his house with a little old kite in his paws. It was a kite his father had made from willow twigs and a torn paper bag he had found on the common. It had a real string to hold it, but the tail was ragged.

'Good-bye, Mother,' called Tim, 'I may fly to the moon. Good-bye.'

'Whatever do you mean?' asked Mrs Rabbit, following him to the doorway on the common. She looked up at the sky and saw the golden brown leaves drifting down and the pale young moon dimly shining.

'I'm going to fly my kite, Mother,' said Tim again. 'Good-bye.'

Mrs Rabbit laughed and watched her son skip down the path and enter the wood. Then she went back to her house, but Tim trundled his soft little feet in the golden leaves, making a sweet sursurring sound, a rustle that fascinated him.

'All these leaves and plenty more on the trees,' he thought. 'I could make a tail for my kite and then I could make – yes, I could – a cloak for my mother.'

He sat down and tossed the leaves in the air and then he drew a heap around him. He fastened a lot of leaves to the kite's bare tail, where the paper had torn away, and soon the kite was ready.

'Now for my mother's cloak,' he muttered. He searched in the gorse bushes for a good sharp needle, and he found some wisps of sheep's wool in the hedge by the field. He 'teased' the wool between his paws to

make a long thread, and he tied this to his needle of gorse. Then he began to stitch the leaves. He worked very hard, making long strings of leaves and joining them together, and he was so intent he did not notice that somebody was watching him. Each little leaf was sewn to another leaf until he had a large web of beech leaves with here and there a nut leaf or an oak leaf with an acorn.

He began to sing in a soft little voice, and somebody listened.

'*Brown leaf, yellow leaf, red and gold,*
Striped leaf and speckled leaf, to keep out the cold.

Tim Rabbit's Magic Cloak

Good little Tim, to make a fine cloak,
Mother will smile and think it's a joke.
Then she will wear it and be a fine lady,
To walk in the fields and woodland shady.'

He heard a little cough and he looked quickly. Watching him was his cousin Sam Hare. 'Oh, Sam. I didn't see you. I thought you were the fox,' he cried.

'If I were a fox I could have eaten you,' said Sam Hare.

'But you are only a hare,' snorted Tim.

'What have you been making, Tim?' asked Sam.

'I've mended my kite and made a cloak for my mother's birthday, to keep her warm in cold weather,' said Tim proudly and he held up the cloak with its brown-gold leaves.

'Oo-oo,' said Sam. 'How clever you are, Tim. I wish – I wish I were clever too.'

'Never mind, Sam. I am, of course, no Ordinary Rabbit! You can fly my kite,' said Tim.

They set off together, Tim holding the cloak and Sam dragging the kite. They left the wood and climbed a little hill. Tim laid the cloak on the ground with a stone on it to say it was private property, and Sam and he ran together holding the kite by its long string.

Sometimes it flopped and danced on the ground, and then it rose up and flew in the air, tugging at the string to get loose.

'Oh, Sam,' cried Tim. 'Suppose it lifted us both up in the air and took us to the moon.'

They ran and ran, but the kite never rose very high, for the wind was half asleep. Suddenly Tim remembered his cloak. He hoped it was safe. So they turned round and ran with the kite to the little hill where they had started. There sat the fox, watching the cloak in a puzzled way.

'Hello, Tim Rabbit,' said the fox, lazily stretching himself. 'Is this your heap of leaves?'

'Yes – yes,' stammered Tim, but Sam Hare hid behind a bush.

'What is it?' asked the fox.

'Only a heap of leaves, and yet it's a cloak for my mother,' said Tim.

'A cloak?' echoed the fox.

'Yes, you wear it like this,' said Tim eagerly, and he picked it up and flung it round his body, so that he was hidden in the folds of red and gold leaves.

'You are invisible,' said the fox slowly.

'Yes,' said Tim, and he started to run, holding the cloak tightly round him and clasping the kite string. The wind lifted the kite and caught the leafy cloak, carrying Tim off his feet. There he was in the air, with his little feet paddling, trying to find the ground.

'Oh, I say. I'm flying,' he cried. 'Oh. Oh.'

'Dear me,' said the fox. 'How remarkable!' He leapt up but he could not reach Tim Rabbit.

Away flew Tim with the wind filling the leafy cloak and tugging at the kite.

'Poof! Poof!' shouted the wind 'Here's a fine cloud of beech leaves,' and it tossed Tim up in the air and swept him far away.

'It's not beech leaves. It's me,' cried Tim, but the wind did not hear as it strode through the sky.

Down below the fox stared, and then he went home. Little Sam Hare came out from behind the bush, and he scampered away to Tim's house.

'Mammy Rabbit!' he called knocking at the door. 'Your Tim has flown away. He's gone towards the moon, Mammy Rabbit.'

Mrs Rabbit began to cry. She went out to the fields and she saw a tiny speck up in the sky. She was sure it was Tim, so she went home and sat down to cry even more.

Tim was enjoying himself as he floated along with the leafy cloak billowing around him, and the kite soaring above. He sang a little song which pleased the wind as it carried this small morsel high above the tree tops

> *'Here I am, up in the sky,*
> *Like a swallow, flying high,*
> *Swept by the wind, held by the cloak,*
> *Fluttering leaves, drifting like smoke.'*

Then Tim glanced down and saw in the distance the great blue sea and the little curling white waves. He felt very frightened and he sang again:

> *'Please Mr Wind, don't let me fall,*
> *I'm only a Rabbit, young and small.*
> *Don't let me tumble down in the sea,*
> *Do take me home to my mother for tea.'*

'A rabbit,' said the wind. 'Tim Rabbit.' It swung

round from north-east, to south, and swept little Tim
Rabbit away from the sea.

It hovered for a few minutes over Tim's home and
then gently dropped Tim, down, down, down, like a
bundle of leaves and fur to the ground.

'Good-bye, Tim,' cried the wind and it blew the
trees and sent showers of leaves to fall over him.

Tim scrambled to his feet, still holding the kite's

string. He ran to the house, kicked the door open and flung himself into his mother's arms.

'Oh, oh,' cried Mrs Rabbit. 'A bundle of leaves? No, it's Tim, my darling lost Tim. Where have you been, Tim? Sam Hare told me you had gone to the moon. And what's this you are wearing?'

'It's your birthday present, Mother,' laughed Tim. 'I made it for you. I made it myself out of a lot of leaves, and, Mother, if you wear it when the wind blows you can fly too.'

'Oh, thank you, Tim,' said Mrs Rabbit. 'This is a lovely cloak. Red and gold and brown, and well sewn. I am proud to wear it. It will keep me warm in the snow.'

She put the cloak round her shoulders and walked about the room with her usual dancing step.

'Brown leaf, yellow leaf, red leaf and gold,
   Striped leaf, and speckled leaf to keep out the cold,'

sang Tim, dancing after her.

'Mother. You are just like a heap of leaves walking in the wind,' said Tim. 'Nobody can spy you. They will think you are only leaves, or maybe a little brown bush.'

Mrs Rabbit threw off the cloak and laughed.

'Leaves walking,' said the fox when a heap of golden leaves rolled past his den one day.

'Leaves talking,' he muttered as he heard a tiny voice sing *'Brown leaf, yellow leaf, red and gold.'*

'There's too much education these days. Leaves talking!' he added crossly. Wise Owl explained that it was a magical cloak, called by a grand name. It was a

'Camoophlaged Cloak', to make something look like something else to save them from bad things.

'Cam-oo-phlaged cloak,' sneezed the fox. 'I should like a cam-oo-phlaged coat myself, striped yellow and brown.'

'Ask Tim Rabbit to make it for you,' said the owl. 'He might, you know.'

The Little Boy
and His House

THERE was once a Little Boy. In the winter he was
TOO COLD. In the summer he was TOO HOT. When it
rained he got WET. And when it was windy he was
NEARLY BLOWN AWAY. So he went to see his uncle.

'I want to build a house,' said the Little Boy.

'In the winter I'm TOO COLD,

'In the summer I'm TOO HOT,

'When it rains I GET WET,

'And when it's windy I'm NEARLY BLOWN AWAY.'

'There was once a time, long ago,' said his Uncle,
'when nobody lived in houses. They found caves and
went to live in them. Perhaps you could find a cave to
live in like they did.'

'But wasn't that very long ago?' said the Little Boy.

'Very, very long ago,' said his Uncle, 'so long ago
that they had no clothes but furs and no tools except
stone ones.'

'Then I don't suppose anyone lives in caves nowa-
days,' said the Little Boy.

'Oh, yes they do,' said his Uncle. 'In Spain some
people live in caves. Much better caves than the old
ones. They have doors that open and shut, and some of
them have windows with glass, and even chimneys.'

'I wonder if they like living in caves,' said the Little

Boy. 'Even with windows and chimneys I should think it might be rather damp and rather dark and rather dirty.'

'Perhaps it might be,' said his Uncle.

'Let's go to Spain and see,' said the Little Boy.

So they did and they found a Spaniard called Don Esteban who lived in a cave ...

'Come inside,' said Don Esteban. So they said, 'Thank you,' and went in, and Don Esteban gave them oranges to eat, and they thought it was very comfort-

able *for a cave*, but after a while the Little Boy said very softly so as not to hurt Don Esteban's feelings: 'I don't like caves. I think houses are better. It is damp – and it is dark – and it is dirty in caves.'

'I think so too,' said his Uncle. So they said 'Goodbye' and came away.

'Perhaps you would like to live in a tent,' said his Uncle. 'Lots of gipsies in England live in tents. They take long, thin sticks and stick them in the ground. Then they bend the tops down and stick *them* in the ground. Then they cover them over with sacks and sometimes they leave a hole in the middle for the smoke to get out.

'When they are tired of one place they put everything on a cart and go somewhere else.'

'Let's go and see,' said the Little Boy, so they walked along the road until they found a gipsy who lived in a tent; he was called Johnnie Faa.

'Come into my tent,' said the gipsy. So they said, 'Thank you,' and went in, and he gave them something to eat which they thought *must* be stewed pheasant, though Johnnie Faa said he didn't think it could be.

But it was a very small tent, and when the Little Boy and his Uncle were inside they could sit down and lie down, but they COULDN'T STAND UP.

'I think these tents are too small,' said the Little Boy very softly, so as not to hurt Johnnie Faa's feelings.

'I think so too,' said his Uncle.

So they said, 'Good-bye,' and came away.

'Aren't there any bigger tents?' said the Little Boy.

'Red Indians have bigger tents,' said his Uncle. 'They live in North America.'

'Let's go to North America,' said the Little Boy, so they went to North America and found some Red Indians who lived in tents.

First the Red Indians put up long poles tied together at the top. Then they covered them with skins and left a sort of chimney for the smoke. The tents had painted pictures on the outside.

The Little Boy and his Uncle put feathers in their hats because they thought that would be polite and they said, 'How do you do?' to an Indian chief who was called Big Bear and who lived in a fine tent called a tepee ...

'Come into my tepee,' said Big Bear. So they said, 'Thank you,' and went in, and he gave them pemmican to eat which is a kind of dried meat. 'It's a lovely tent,' said the Little Boy. 'I'd like to live in a tent like this.'

But just then the wind began to blow and it BLEW and BLEW and BLEW and at last the tent was blown over.

'I think houses are better than tents,' said the Little Boy very softly, so as not to hurt Big Bear's feelings.

'I think so too,' said his Uncle, so they said, 'Goodbye' and came away.

'Would you like to live on a boat?' said the Little Boy's Uncle. 'In China a great many people live on the rivers in boats.'

'I think that's a very good idea,' said the Little Boy. 'When you are tired of one place you can sail away to another. I think I should like to live on a boat. Let's go to China and see the people who live on boats.'

So they went to China and found it was a very, very big country and full of people.

And there they found a man who lived on a boat with his wife and *his* little boy. His name was Wang Fu and he wore a straw coat to keep the rain off and a simply enormous straw hat.

The Little Boy and his Uncle also put on big Chinese hats and went to see the boat in which Wang Fu lived with his wife and his little boy. And they found it was a lovely boat with a house on it which had a roof of straw matting.

And Wang Fu said, 'Come on board.' So they said, 'Thank you' and went on board, and found it very comfortable, with tables and chairs, and curtains to let down when the sun got too hot. Wang Fu gave them tea to drink.

'It's a lovely boat,' said the Little Boy. But just then a storm began and the waves were very big and the boat tossed about horribly.

'I don't think I should like to live on a boat always,' said the Little Boy very softly, so that Wang Fu shouldn't hear.

'I don't think I should like it either,' said his Uncle. So they said, 'Good-bye' and came away.

'Why not try SNOW?' said the Little Boy's Uncle.

'Snow!' said the Little Boy. 'However do you make houses of snow?'

'I don't know,' said his Uncle, 'but near the North Pole there are Eskimos who live in snow houses and they are supposed to be very warm and snug inside, so warm that Eskimos take off most of their clothes when they go indoors.'

'Let's go and see,' said the Little Boy.

So they went near the North Pole where there was a lot of snow and ice both on the land and on the sea, and there they found an Eskimo called E-took-a-shoo building a snow house.

'How do you build snow houses?' said the Little Boy and his Uncle together.

'Like this,' said E-took-a-shoo. 'You cut big blocks of hard snow and put them one on top of another and when you've finished you pour water over it and that freezes and it all becomes as hard as a stone.'

'Come inside,' said E-took-a-shoo. So they said,

'Thank you,' and went in, and E-took-a-shoo gave them blubber to eat, which was very like very, very fat bacon.

Soon the weather grew warmer and the house began to melt.

'Oh, dear!' said E-took-a-shoo. 'Soon it will be summer and we'll have to live in tents like Red Indians.'

'I want a house I can live in all the year round,' said

the Little Boy very softly, so as not to hurt E-took-a-shoo's feelings.

'Then a snow house won't do,' said his Uncle. So they said 'Good-bye' and came away.

'Black men in Africa build houses of GRASS AND STICKS,' said the Little Boy's Uncle.

'Is it hot in Africa?' said the Little Boy.

'Yes,' said his Uncle.

'Then let's go there,' said the Little Boy.

So they went to Africa and it was VERY HOT INDEED and they found a black man called M'popo who was building a house of grass and sticks.

First he tied a lot of sticks together to make a framework for his house and then he put bundles of long, dry grass all over the top and tied it on carefully, so that the wind would not blow it away.

Then he put long, dry grass all round the sides and tied *that* on carefully and so the roof and the walls were finished.

'That's a beautiful house,' said the Little Boy, and M'popo was very pleased.

'Come inside,' said M'popo. So they said, 'Thank you,' and went in, and he gave them bananas to eat.

'The walls are only made of grass,' said the Little Boy. 'What do you do when it's freezing cold weather?'

'It never is freezing cold here,' said M'popo.

'But it's often freezing cold where I live, so I don't think a grass house would do,' said the Little Boy very softly, so as not to hurt M'popo's feelings.

'I don't think it would,' said his Uncle. So they said, 'Good-bye' and came away.

'M'popo has a cousin called M'toto,' said the Little Boy's Uncle, 'who lives not so very far away in a house with very, very *thick* walls of MUD.'

'However do you make walls of mud?' said the Little Boy.

'Let's go and ask M'toto,' said his Uncle.

So they went to the town where M'toto lived and found it was all built of mud houses. In the middle was a mosque (where M'toto said his prayers) which had a queer tower with pieces of wood sticking out of it.

'However do you make houses of mud?' asked the Little Boy.

'It's easy to make mud houses,' said M'toto. 'You make the walls of nice sticky clay and the hot sun of Africa dries it hard as hard. Then you put sticks across for the roof, and mats on the sticks, and more nice sticky clay, and the hot sun dries *that* as hard as hard, and there you are.'

'Come inside,' said M'toto. So they said, 'Thank you,' and went in, and he gave them dates to eat.

But just then it began to RAIN. It RAINED and RAINED and half M'toto's house was washed away.

'It often rains where I live; I don't think a mud house would do for me,' said the Little Boy very softly, so as not to hurt M'toto's feelings.

'I don't think it would,' said his Uncle, so they said 'Good-bye' and came away.

'I wonder if you could make a house of STONES,' said the Little Boy's Uncle.

'Where do they make stone houses?' said the Little Boy.

'All sorts of places,' said his Uncle.

'What's one of them?' said the Little Boy.

'The West of Ireland,' said his Uncle.

'Let's go there,' said the Little Boy.

So they did, and they found an Irishman called Mr Michael O'Flaherty building a house of stones.

He piled the stones up very cleverly to make the walls and the chimney, and he put big bits of wood across to make the roof, and he put dry grass on top, and soon the house was ready.

The house had a queer kind of door. It was in two

pieces; when you shut the bottom piece then sheep and cows and hens couldn't get in, and when you shut it all then nobody could get in.

'Come inside,' said Mr Michael O'Flaherty. So they said, 'Thank you,' and went in, and he gave them an Irish stew made of mutton and potatoes.

'Where do you get all these stones?' said the Little Boy.

'Aren't they lying about all over the fields?' said Mr Michael O'Flaherty.

'Not where I live,' said the Little Boy.

'Isn't that a shame now?' said Mr Michael O'Flaherty. 'You could never be building this kind of house.'

'No, I'm afraid not,' said the Little Boy. So they said 'Good-bye' and came away.

'What about WOOD?' said the Little Boy's Uncle. 'In Sweden they make houses of wood. Everybody except Don Esteban and E-took-a-shoo uses some wood in his house, but in Sweden they use hardly anything else.'

'Let's go and see,' said the Little Boy.

So they went to Sweden and found a Swede called Lars Larsson making a house.

'Is it all made of wood?' said the Little Boy.

'All but the chimney,' said Lars Larsson. 'We make that of stones or brick, but everything else is wood. We make the walls of big trees and cut notches in them so that they fit together properly and the roof is made of thin pieces of wood over-lapping.'

'Come inside,' said Lars Larsson. So they said, 'Thank you' and went in, and Lars Larsson gave them smoked salmon to eat, and everything was made of wood, carved and painted, even the dishes and bowls were made of wood.

'What a lot of trees you must need!' said the Little Boy.

41

'You see we live in a forest,' said Lars Larsson.

'But I don't,' said the Little Boy.

'Then it would be difficult to build this sort of house,' said Lars Larsson.

So they said 'Good-bye' and came away.

'WHAT A LOT OF DIFFERENT WAYS OF BUILDING HOUSES!' said the Little Boy. 'But how shall I build MINE?'

'Let's try BRICKS,' said his Uncle. 'We'll get clay and sand and mix them together and make it into square bricks all the same size and shape.'

So they did.

'What do we do now?' said the Little Boy.

'Wait till the bricks are dry,' said his Uncle.

So they waited and waited until at last they were dry.

'Now,' said his Uncle, 'we must put the bricks in a pile and light a fire underneath.'

So they did and the bricks were all baked as hard as stones and turned the most beautiful red colour.

'Now we must get some lime,' said the Little Boy's Uncle. 'It's a special sort of stone that has been burnt until it's a white powder, and you mix it with water and sand and that makes the mortar to stick the bricks together with.'

So they did. And then the mortar was ready.

'Now,' said the Little Boy, 'LET'S START BUILDING!'

'What shall we put on the roof?' said the Little Boy.

'There's THATCH and TILES and SLATES,' said his Uncle. 'Thatch is just dry straw or reeds, and slates are very thin pieces of a special sort of stone, and tiles are like very, very thin bricks.'

'I don't know which would be best,' said the Little Boy.

'I don't know either,' said his Uncle.

And in the end they decided to toss up, but since a penny has only two sides, they said, 'Eena, Meena, Mina, Mo' instead, and it cames out TILES.

So they made a lot of tiles from clay mixed with

sand and left them to dry and then baked them just as they had baked the bricks, and when they were ready they put them on the roof so that each tile overlapped the one below it.

Then they put a green bush on the chimney to let everyone know that the house was finished.

And the Little Boy and his Uncle asked all their friends. They asked:

Don Esteban, the Spaniard,
            and
Johnnie Faa, the gipsy,
            and
Big Bear, the Red Indian,
            and

Wang Fu from China,
> and

E-took-a-shoo, the Eskimo,
> and

M'popo
> and

M'toto, the black men from Africa,
> and

Mr Michael O'Flaherty from Ireland,
> and

Lars Larsson from Sweden;

and they all came with their wives to see the house that the Little Boy and his Uncle had built.

At last they all arrived at the house. E-took-a-shoo thought it a very hot place and M'popo and M'toto thought it very cold. Lars Larsson thought it odd there weren't more trees, and Big Bear thought it odd there were so many. Don Esteban was surprised that there weren't any rocks and caves, and Mr Michael O'Flaherty was surprised that stones didn't lie about all over the fields. Wang Fu thought it very odd to live on dry land. Only Johnny Faa wasn't surprised. He'd been there before; he'd been everywhere.

And they all stood in the garden and admired the Little Boy's house, but they left their animals outside the gate for fear they would trample on the beautiful new gravel path. And when everyone had admired the outside, they all went in at the front door and hung up their hats in the hall – all except M'popo who hadn't a hat.

And the Little Boy gave them cream buns and crumpets and ices to eat, and they liked them very much. (E-took-a-shoo was particularly fond of the ices.) And they thought the Little Boy's house was lovely because ...

When it was cold he was WARM. When it was hot he was COOL. When it rained he was DRY. And when it was windy he was SHELTERED.

And they all went home determined to build brick houses like the one the Little Boy had built.

But when they all got home again, Don Esteban thought that after all it *was* very convenient to have a cave all ready made for you, and Johnnie Faa and Big Bear thought how convenient it was to have a house you could carry about wherever you wanted to go, and Wang Fu thought it was even more convenient to have a house that would carry *you* about. And E-took-a-shoo saw that where he lived he would *have* to build with ice and snow because there was nothing else, and M'popo and M'toto saw that they would *have* to build with grass and mud because they had nothing else, and Mr Michael O'Flaherty thought that if you had a lot of stones lying about the fields it was a shame not to use them, and Lars Larsson thought the same about the trees in the forest.

So
    what
       do
          you
             think
               they
                 did?

THEY ALL WENT ON BUILDING JUST AS THEY'D ALWAYS DONE, FOR WHAT THEY ALL SAID WAS ...

 'It depends ...

  'It all depends ...

   'It all depends on WHERE YOU LIVE and WHAT YOU HAVE TO BUILD WITH.'

The Ossopit Tree

ONE terribly hot summer in the forests of Africa there was a great shortage of anything to eat. The animals had been hunting around here, there and everywhere and had finally eaten up the very last twig and root. They were very hungry indeed.

Suddenly they came upon a wonderful-looking tree, hung with the most tempting, juicy-looking fruit. But, of course, they didn't know whether the fruit was safe to eat or not because they had no idea what its name was. And they simply had to know its name. Luckily they did know that the tree belonged to an old lady called Jemma. So they decided to send the hare, their fastest runner, to ask her what the name of the tree was.

Off went the hare as fast as his legs could carry him and he found old Jemma in front of her hut.

'Oh, Mrs Jemma,' he said. 'We animals are dying of hunger. If you could only tell us the name of that wonderful tree of yours you could save us all from starving.'

'Gladly I will do that,' answered Jemma. 'It's perfectly safe to eat the fruit. Its name is OSSOPIT.'

'Oh,' said the hare, 'that's a very difficult name. I shall forget it by the time I get back.'

'No, it's really quite easy,' said Jemma. 'Just think of "opposite" and then sort of say it backwards, like this:

opposite – OSSOPIT.'

'Oh, thanks very much,' said the hare, and off he scampered.

As he ran he kept muttering, 'opposite, ottipis, ossipit' and got all mixed up. So that when he got back to the other animals all he could say was, 'Well, Jemma

did tell me the name but I can't remember whether it's ossipit, ottipis, or ossupit. I do know it's got something to do with "opposite".'

'Oh dear,' they all sighed. 'We had better send someone with a better memory.'

'I'll go,' said the goat. 'I never forget anything.' So he headed straight for Jemma's hut, grunting and snorting all the way.

'I'm sorry to bother you again, Mrs Jemma,' he panted, 'but that stupid hare couldn't remember the name of the tree. Do you mind telling it me once more?'

'Gladly I will,' replied the old woman. 'It's OSSOPIT. Just think of "opposite" and then sort of say it backwards:

opposite – OSSOPIT.'

'Rightee-oh,' said the goat, 'and thank you very much, I'm sure.'

And off he galloped, fast as he could, kicking up clouds of dust, and all the way he kept saying:

'Ottopis, oppossit, possitto, otto ...' until he got back.

'I know the name of that tree,' he said. 'It's oppitis, n ... no ... ossipit, n ... no ... otup ... oh dear ... I just can't get it right.'

'Well, who can we send this time?' they all asked. They didn't want to bother old Jemma again.

'I'm perfectly willing to have a go,' piped up a young sparrow. 'I'll be back in no time,' and with a whisk of his tail he had flown off before anyone could stop him.

'Good morrow, gentle Jemma,' he said. 'Could you please tell me the name of that tree just *once* more. Hare and goat just could *not* get it right.'

'Right gladly I will,' said old Jemma patiently. 'It's OSSOPIT, OSS-O-PIT. It's a wee bit difficult but just think of "opposite" and then sort of say it backwards:

opposite – OSSOPIT.'

'I'm most grateful, madam,' said the sparrow and flew off twittering to himself: 'opposite, ossitup, ottu-

pus, oissopit,' until he finally got back to his famishing friends.

'Do tell us, sparrow,' they all cried.

'Yes,' chirped the sparrow. 'It's definitely "ossitup", n ... no ... oittusip, n ... no ... oippisuit ... Oh dear, I give up. So very sorry.'

By now the animals were desperate. Just imagine them all sitting round the gorgeous tree and unable to pick any of its mouth-watering fruit.

Suddenly up spoke the tortoise. 'I shall go,' he said. 'I know it will take a bit of time but I will not forget the name once I've been told. My family has the finest reputation in the world for good memories.'

'No,' they moaned. 'You are too slow. We shall all be dead by the time you get back.'

'Why not let me take tortoise on my back?' asked the zebra. 'I'm hopeless at remembering things but my speed is second to none. I'll have him back here in no time at all.' They all thought this was a splendid idea and so off raced the zebra with the tortoise clinging to his back.

'Good morning, Madam Jemma,' said the tortoise. 'I'm sorry I have no time to alight. But if we don't get the name of that tree most of us will be dead by tonight. That's why I've come on zebra's back. He's a bit faster than I am, you know.'

'Yes, I rather think he is,' smiled old Jemma benignly.

'Well, it's OSSOPIT. Just think of "opposite" and then sort of say it backwards, like this: opposite – oss-o-pit.'

'Just let me repeat it three times before I go,' said the tortoise, 'just to see if I get it right.' And then he said it, very, very slowly, deliberately and loudly, and nodding his tiny head at each syllable:

'OSS-O-PIT OSS-O-PIT OSS-O-PIT.'

'Bravo!' said Jemma, 'you'll never forget it now.'

And she was right.

The zebra thudded back hot foot and the tortoise was never in any doubt that he had the name right at last.

'It's OSS-O-PIT,' he announced to his ravenous friends.

'Ossopit, ossopit, ossopit,' they all cried. 'It's an ossopit tree, and it's perfectly safe to eat.' And they all helped themselves to the wonderful fruit. You just can't imagine how delicious it tasted.

And to show how grateful they were, they appointed the tortoise their Chief Adviser on Important Matters (he has C.A.I.M. after his name). And he still is Chief Adviser to this very day.

Johnny Appleseed

MANY years ago, when your grandfather's great-grand-father was still a child, there lived a boy in Boston in America called John Chapman. He loved the country-side, the flowers and trees and woods, and he knew all about the beasts and birds who lived in them. His favourite tree was the apple-tree. He loved climbing apple-trees and munching an apple as he rested on their branches.

Once as he was happily chewing a juicy apple he picked out a few of the little brown apple-pips and gazed at them thoughtfully.

'If I planted these seeds,' he said aloud, 'the whole countryside would be filled with apple-trees.' So when he grew to be a man, John Chapman started roaming the country with a large sack full of apple-seeds on his back and a cooking-pan slung round his shoulder. He would stop every now and then and plant a seed or give a handful to a passer-by. He was so happy and friendly that he became known to everyone for miles around. People would give him food and shelter in return for his apple-pips and they called him Johnny Appleseed.

Soon he roamed farther and farther away from his home town, planting apple-seeds wherever he went. He planted his seeds up and down the country, in the bare brown earth in the autumn.

After the winter the spring came and Johnny Apple-

seed would go back to each place to see the little green
shoots pushing up through the earth.

Everywhere baby apple-trees sprang up and grew.
In time they would blossom and bear fruit, and his
eyes twinkled with happiness when he thought of all
the children who would one day enjoy all those wonderful apples – the Pippins and the Russets and the
Pound Sweets as well as the baked apples and apple-
jellies and toffee-apples they would provide.

On his wanderings Johnny Appleseed always slept in
the open air and cooked his own meals. He met many
wolves, foxes, deer and even bears and made friends
with them all. Even when it snowed he slept out in the
open and showed no fear. Rather than send away a bear
and her cub from the hollow log where they were
sheltering, he preferred to remain in the cold.

But one day in the bitter winter when snow covered
all the beloved apple-trees which he had planted, he
caught a chill and was very ill. A mother bear and her
cub watched him sadly as he lay, and then wandered
off. Luckily some Indians saw the bears and followed
their trail till it led them to where Johnny Appleseed
lay. They at once recognized him as their old friend
who had planted the wonderful seeds in their land.
They took him to their tepee and gave him their
medicines and they gave him good food and they
looked after him with tender care.

Then one sunny morning Johnny Appleseed opened
his eyes and smiled at his faithful Indian friends. He
knew they had saved his life. He wandered out into the
fields. The snow had melted from the apple-trees and

in the early spring their fragrant blossoms gleamed in the sun.

Johnny was now determined to wander even farther but he always returned to visit old friends and especially the Indians who had saved his life. On and on he went, tramping hundreds of miles along riversides, up hill and down dale, planting the brown pips wherever he went.

The years rolled by and Johnny Appleseed was now an old man with long white hair and flowing beard. But his cheeks were rosy from the fresh air and wind and his black eyes always twinkled with joy and kindness.

Children would gather round to hear the stories of his wanderings and wherever he went the settlers in this new land knew him as the man who made their countryside rich with beautiful trees where once there was nothing but the bare brown earth.

Pierre

*a cautionary tale in Five Chapters
and a Prologue*

Prologue

There once was a boy
named Pierre
who only would say,
'I don't care!'
Read his story,
my friend,
for you'll find
at the end
that a suitable
moral lies there.

Chapter 1

One day
his mother said
when Pierre
climbed out of bed,
'Good morning,
darling boy,
you are
my only joy.'

Pierre

Pierre said,
'I don't care!'
'What would you
like to eat?'
'I don't care!'
'Some lovely
cream of wheat?'
'I don't care!'
'Don't sit backwards
on your chair.'

'I don't care!'
'Or pour syrup
on your hair.'
'I don't care!'
'You are acting
like a clown.'

'I don't care!'
'And we have
to go to town.'
'I don't care!'
'Don't you want
to come, my dear?'
'I don't care!'
'Would you rather
stay right here?'
'I don't care!'
So his mother
left him there.

Chapter 2

His father said,
'Get off your head
or I will march you
up to bed!'
Pierre said,
'I don't care!'
'I would think
that you could see –'
'I don't care!'
'Your head is where
your feet should be!'
'I don't care!'
'If you keep standing
upside down –'
'I don't care!'
'We'll never ever
get to town.'
'I don't care!'
'If only you would
say I CARE.'
'I don't care!'
'I'd let you fold
the folding chair.'
So his parents left him there.
They didn't take him
anywhere.

Pierre

Chapter 3

Now, as the night
began to fall
a hungry lion
paid a call.
He looked Pierre
right in the eye
and asked him
if he'd like to die.
Pierre said,
'I don't care!'
'I can eat you,
don't you see?'
'I don't care!'
'And you will be
inside of me.'
'I don't care!'
'Then you'll never
have to bother —'
'I don't care!'
'With a mother
and a father.'
'I don't care!'
'Is that all
you have to say?'
'I don't care!'
'Then I'll eat you,
if I may.'
'I don't care!'
So the lion
ate Pierre.

Chapter 4

Arriving home
at six o'clock,
his parents had
a dreadful shock!
They found the lion
sick in bed
and cried,
'Pierre is surely dead!'
They pulled the lion
by the hair.
They hit him
with the folding chair.
His mother asked,
'Where is Pierre?'
The lion answered,
'I don't care!'
His father said,
'Pierre's in there!'

Chapter 5

They rushed the lion
into town.
The doctor shook him
up and down.
And when the lion
gave a roar –
Pierre fell out
upon the floor.

He rubbed his eyes
and scratched his head
and laughed
because he wasn't dead.
His mother cried
and held him tight.
His father asked,
'Are you all right?'
Pierre said,
'I am feeling fine,
please take me home,
it's half past nine.'
The lion said,
'If you would care
to climb on me,
I'll take you there.'
Then everyone
looked at Pierre
who shouted,
'Yes, indeed I care ! !'
The lion took them
home to rest
and stayed on
as a week-end guest.

The moral of Pierre
is: CARE !

The House in the Forest

ONCE upon a time there was a woodcutter who lived with his wife and three daughters, Gerda, Lisa and Gretel, on the edge of a lonely forest. One morning as he was setting off to work, he said to his wife: 'See that Gerda brings my dinner to the forest, because I shall have no time to come home. I will strew some millet seed along the road so that she will not lose her way.'

At noon Gerda left the house carrying a basket with her father's dinner. But the birds in the forest had pecked all the millet seed and very soon Gerda had lost the path her father had traced for her. Still she continued on her way till the sun set and everything became dark and you could hear nothing except the frightening screeching of the owls and the whistling of the wind in the trees.

Suddenly she saw a light in the distance. 'That must be a cottage,' she said to herself. 'I will go and ask for a night's rest.' She walked warily up and knocked at the door. A gruff voice called out, 'Come in.'

She stepped into the room to find a very, very old man, white-haired and sitting still as a statue by the table, his chin resting on his hands and his white beard nearly touching the floor. In the corner, near the stove, sat a cow, a cock and a hen.

'Could you please give me shelter for the night,'

asked Gerda. The old man did not reply but turning
slowly to the three animals said:

> '*Is it nay*
> *Or is it yea,*
> *Shall the little lady stay?*'

All three gave a long, slow nod.

'Very well, then,' said the old man, 'you may have
some food and spend the night here. Pray go into the
kitchen and prepare supper.'

Gerda found plenty of food in the kitchen and made
herself a good meal which she carried to the table and
ate heartily, not offering anything either to the old man
or to the animals.

When she had finished, she asked the old man:
'Where is my bed?' He replied: 'You will find two
beds upstairs and fresh linen. So kindly make them

up.' But Gerda only made one of the beds and went to sleep without any further thought for the old man. Soon after, he came up and found her fast asleep. Sadly he shook his head, opened a trapdoor in the floor and let the bed down into the cellar below.

That evening the woodman returned to his house, very angry with his wife. 'You have let me go hungry all day,' he said.

'It's not my fault,' said his wife. 'Gerda must have lost her way. I do hope she'll be back soon.'

The next morning the woodman set to work in the forest again. 'You had better send Lisa with my dinner today,' he told his wife. 'I'll spread some lentils along the path; they are bigger than millet seeds, so she won't lose her way.'

Lisa set off at noon, but when she tried to follow the path she could not see lentils at all, for the birds had pecked them all. She wandered this way and that until it got quite dark and she became very frightened. Then she espied a light far away and she soon found herself knocking at the door of the old man's cottage. She asked for shelter and again the old man turned to the three animals and asked:

> '*Is it nay*
> *Or is it yea,*
> *Shall the little lady stay?*'

They gave a long, slow nod and the old man told Lisa to prepare a meal in the kitchen – which she did, just as Gerda had done. She then brought it to the table and ate heartily, never giving a thought to the old man or to the three animals. When she had finished, she asked him: 'Where am I to sleep?'

The old man told her about the two beds and the fresh linen upstairs and asked her to go and make them up. Soon after he followed her up and found her fast asleep; only one bed had been made. He shook his head sadly, opened the trap door and let her down into the cellar below.

That evening, when the woodman returned home from work, he was terribly angry.

'No dinner again, wife,' he grumbled. And his wife, very puzzled, said: 'I can't think what can have gone wrong. Lisa must have lost her way too. I do hope nothing has happened to them.'

But the next morning the woodman had to set off to the forest again.

'Now, do make sure that Gretel brings me my dinner in good time today,' he said.

'But I don't want my youngest daughter to get lost in the woods,' his wife protested. 'Let me bring it myself.'

'No,' said the woodman firmly. 'Gretel is a very sensible child. *She* won't get lost like the others. And this time I will strew the path with peas.'

So at midday Gretel set off with a basket containing her father's dinner on her arm. But she could find no peas at all along the path; the hungry birds had eaten every single one. The poor girl was most upset, thinking how anxious her mother would be if she did not return home very soon. It was not long before it became quite dark and she was relieved to see a light in the distance.

It came from the same cottage that her two sisters had found.

She politely asked the old man whether it would be too much trouble to put her up for the night. He turned his white-bearded face towards the animals and asked:

> '*Is it nay*
> *Or is it yea,*
> *Shall the little lady stay?*'

Once again they all gave a long, slow nod. When the old man told her to go into the kitchen to prepare a meal, Gretel said: 'Thank you most kindly, sir, but first I will fetch some food for your three animals.' She went outside and brought in some corn for the cock and hen and an armful of hay for the cow. Then she fetched a big bowl of water to quench their thirst. While the animals were happily eating, she went into the kitchen. It was not very long before she came back with two plates of very tasty-looking food, one for the old man and one for herself. When they finished, the old man asked Gretel to make up the two beds upstairs.

Gretel was very tired after the day's wanderings and was fast asleep when the old man followed her up shortly afterwards. But he was very happy to see that the other bed had been made, and he, too, was soon fast asleep in it.

In the middle of the night, Gretel was awakened by all sorts of strange noises. Doors kept creaking and slamming, the beams under the ceiling trembled and the stairs swayed like a boat on the open sea. And then

– a tremendous crash. Then all was quiet. Gretel fell fast
asleep again.

In the morning when she opened her eyes, an amazing sight greeted her and she thought she was dreaming.

She was in a magnificent silken nightgown and the beds
were covered with luxurious satin counterpanes. The
sunlit bedroom was huge and blue velvet drapings
hung around the bed. When she had recovered a
little from her astonishment, Gretel's first thought was
for the old man. 'I must get up and cook him some

breakfast,' she murmured to herself. 'And I must also feed the hen, the cock and the cow.' But no sooner was she out of bed than she saw a handsome young man sleeping peacefully in the other bed. As she stood staring in thrilled amazement, the young man awoke and sat up.

'Do not be alarmed,' he said. 'I am the king's son. I was changed by a wicked witch into a white-haired old man and condemned to live in this cottage. My three faithful servants were changed into a cow, a cock and a hen.' At that very moment in walked three servants clad in rich red livery. 'Why, here they are!' exclaimed the prince, overjoyed.

'And now,' he continued, turning to Gretel, 'you have broken the witch's spell by your kindness to me and the animals. The cottage has been changed back into a royal palace and you shall be my royal bride.'

Gretel's mother and father were summoned to the wedding feast and Gerda and Lisa, who had been taught a bitter lesson, were freed from the cellar, and so they all lived happily ever after.

A Drink of Water

I T was a terribly hot day in the jungle, and all the birds and beasts, exhausted from the heat, had curled up to sleep. The silence was broken only by an occasional snapping of twigs and beating of soft-feathered wings as a parrot nearly slipped off its perch in a tall tree.

The only creature who couldn't sleep was a small brown monkey, who was very very thirsty indeed. He wandered on all fours through the lush green under-growth in the hope of finding a small puddle. Every now and then he stopped and raised himself on to his back legs, peering this way and that for a tell-tale sparkle of sunlight on water. But it was useless, for it had been a very very long, hot, dry summer.

At last his search led him to the edge of the dark green jungle, to the place where the desert begins. He stopped again, blinking into the strong sunlight. But he knew that there was no chance at all of finding cool water in the desert.

But what was that he could see? Out there, standing all by itself, was a tall, fat pot – just the sort of pot which might be expected to have water in it. With a bound the monkey was beside it. If he climbed on to a dead branch among the stones he could just manage to peer into the darkness inside of the pot. Was there water in it? He couldn't see any water, but then, it was very dark in there. Gingerly he lowered a thin arm into the pot. His long sensitive fingers could feel a coolness which might mean that there was water farther down. So he very carefully lowered his hand farther, and farther, and farther, until he was standing on tiptoe and his arm was stretched as far as it would go. And then the very tips of his long fingers felt cold water.

And now what was he to do, may I ask? Just think: the water was so near, and yet so hard to reach!

'I will put my shoulder to the pot,' said the small brown monkey, gently scratching his lower lip with a long finger, 'and I will rock it until it tumbles over – and then I will drink the water.' And he put his thin bony shoulder against the pot, and pushed with all his might. Then he pushed again and again and again until – the pot began to rock. It rocked very little at first but gradually it swayed more and more and it seemed that the very next push would send it toppling over.

'Stop!' called a small voice. The small brown monkey stopped in surprise, and the pot gently rocked itself to a standstill. There was no one to be seen.

'Who said that?' asked the small brown monkey.

'I did,' said a green lizard, sliding quickly from beneath the pot and raising his head towards the monkey. 'I live under this pot and I was trying to have a nap when you came and started making the ground shake. And why are you wearing that fur on a hot day like this?'

The monkey did not answer the last question and looked very ashamed.

'I am sorry to disturb you,' he said, 'but I wanted to drink that cool water. I can't reach it and so I must spill it on the ground before I can drink it.'

'Really, you ought to have more sense,' said the lizard. 'Just look at the ground.' And he whisked round in a flash, so that one moment he was facing one way and the next he was facing the other. 'It's all hot stone and dry dust,' he went on. 'If you spill the water then the ground will drink it all up before you could get a single drop. Think of something else and have the goodness to make less noise about it when other people are sleeping.' And with that he darted under the pot once more.

The small brown monkey sat down on the stones of the desert and looked at the pot again, and felt thirstier than ever.

He had been sitting for a few minutes with the sun

beating down on him, when suddenly he felt cold. He noticed that he was now sitting in shadow, and looking up he saw a great black shape hovering over him.

'Who's that?' asked the monkey.

'I am a monkey-eating eagle,' said the big shape, coming nearer, 'and who are you?'

Now the small brown monkey knew what was good for him, and fortunately he was clever enough to have an answer ready. 'By a strange coincidence,' he replied quickly, 'I am an eagle-eating monkey, and I should be pleased to meet you.'

The big bird hastily rose several feet higher into the blue sky.

'Have you by any chance,' called the small brown monkey after him, 'seen any water in your travels?'

'From up here I can see everything,' came the reply, 'and the only water that I can see is the hippopotamus's pond.' With that the great bird rose higher still. 'Second on the left past the mango tree and first right after the paw-paw tree.' And with that the great bird soared up and up until it disappeared in the sky.

It was a hot and thirsty little monkey who trudged back into the stuffy green heat of the jungle. He followed the directions given to him, and at last arrived at the hippopotamus's pond. But what a disappointment awaited him! Instead of cool, fresh water, as he had hoped, there was thick, steaming, muddy water.

'Ugh! I can't drink that!' said the sad creature, and he squatted down on his hind quarters and cried.

Now the hippopotamus had seen and heard all this from her position in the middle of the pool. But because she was almost completely under the water (all except her eyes and her nostrils) the monkey hadn't noticed her. At first she had kept quite still because she had been a little offended – I may as well admit it – by the monkey's unwillingness to drink her beautiful bath-water. However, she was a tender-hearted old thing and

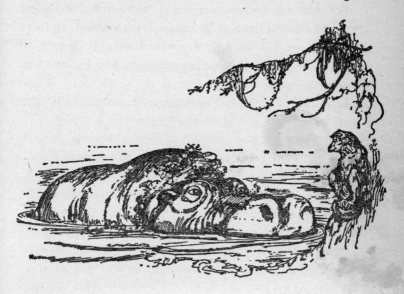

as soon as the monkey began to cry, she floated to the surface and, garlanded with smelly pond-weed, swam to the bank.

'There, there,' she said comfortingly. 'Did you want a drink, then?'

The monkey looked up quickly and gazed at the large smiling face which greeted him. In fact, he rather forgot his manners and *stared* at it, fascinated by the bristles on her chin. But he quickly remembered himself and said: 'Good afternoon. Yes, I would very much like a drink, because I'm so hot and thirsty.'

'Then just wait for me to climb out and I'll help you search through the jungle for water,' said the hippopotamus.

It was such a well-meant and kind offer that the monkey felt he had to accept it, although he knew that apart from the water in the pot, which he couldn't reach, there wasn't a single drop in the whole jungle.

So he waited for the hippopotamus to come out of the pond and she did. And what do you think! The monkey noticed, with his eyes wide open with delight, that as she climbed out of the pond, the level of the water slowly went down.

'Oh, please get in again!' called the monkey excitedly.

'But I want to help you,' insisted the hippopotamus.

'And so you will!' cried the small brown monkey.

With a puzzled look on her huge face, but nevertheless pleased to be useful, the hippopotamus sank slowly back into the water. Sure enough, as she did so the water rose again in the pond.

'Hurrah!' shouted the monkey, bounding away. Then remembering his manners again, he bounded back and said quietly: 'Thank you very much for helping me. I am most grateful to you.' And he ran off to the edge of the jungle.

Back at the pot he quickly collected an armful of big stones – the biggest he could find. He carried them to the side of the pot, climbed up on to the branch, and began to drop the stones in, ever so gently, one by one.

'Splash!' went the first one, faintly, as it hit the bottom.

'Splash!' went the next, a little louder.

And he dropped in more and more until the big pot was three-quarters filled with stones and – what do you think? – the water had risen to the very brim. All the monkey had to do then was to purse his lips and drink the fresh, cool water from the top of the pot.

'And when the water gets too low again,' he said happily to himself, 'I can always drop some more stones in.'

It's a clever monkey who uses his eyes and his common sense.

Jacoble Tells the Truth

ONCE there was old Jacob and little Jacoble – and they they had seven little lambs to take care of. One fine day they were on their way home. The sun still shone brightly. The seven little lambs thought of the wonderful green grass they had eaten for lunch. Old Jacob was thinking of how thankful one must be for such a fine day. And little Jacoble ... he did not know ... what to think ... until he thought a wonderful idea, and he cried, 'Jacob, oh, Jacob! Do you know what I saw yesterday? I saw a green rabbit flying in the air and it was so big – bigger than an elephant!'

'Of course you saw that with your own eyes,' said old Jacob.

'Of course I did,' said Jacoble, and he was all proud.

'It's a good thing you really saw that big flying green rabbit. Because if you hadn't' – said old Jacob – 'that bridge we are going to go over is a very strange one. As soon as anyone who hasn't told the truth crosses it, the bridge breaks in two under his feet.'

Then they walked on.

'Ja-cob,' said Jacoble a little later. 'You know that big green flying rabbit I saw yesterday ... Well, it wasn't really flying, and ... it wasn't quite as big as an elephant ... But it was very big. It was just about the size of a horse. Of a young horse!'

'Big as a horse?' asked old Jacob, as they came nearer

and nearer the bridge, and little Jacoble began not to feel so well.

'Jacob, oh Jacob,' said Jacoble. 'That big green rabbit I saw yesterday – I had something in my eye – so I couldn't see very well. It wasn't such an awfully big rabbit after all. But it was green. Yes, that's what it was – all green!'

Old Jacob didn't say a word. He just walked over the bridge. But Jacoble didn't follow him. He was very frightened. Little Jacoble just stood at the edge of the bridge. He had good reason to be frightened. 'Jacob,' he said. 'Oh, Jacob! You know that rabbit I saw yesterday. It wasn't green. No, no. It was just a little brown rabbit.'

Then he didn't feel frightened any more ... and he ran happily over the bridge.

The Two Giants

ONCE, long ago, two Giants lived in a beautiful country. In summer it was warm, and in winter the land was even more beautiful under snow.

Each day the Giants walked together among the mountains and through the forests, taking care not to step on the trees. Birds made nests in their beards, and everywhere the Giants went thrushes and nightingales sang.

One day while paddling in the sea, the two Giants found a pink shell. The shell was very bright and both Giants admired it.

'It will look lovely on a string round my neck,' said the Giant called Boris.

'Oh no! It will be on a string round *my* neck,' said Sam, the other Giant, 'and it will look better there.'

For the first time in their lives they began to argue. And as they did the sun went behind a cloud and the cloud became bigger and blacker. The wind blew and blew and the waves and clouds grew and grew. It began to rain. The more the Giants argued, the colder the day became. The waves swept higher and higher up the beach.

Boris and Sam began hurriedly pulling on their socks. Before they could put their shoes on, a huge wave completely covered the beach.

The wave swept away the shoes and the shell

The Giants were furious and threw stones at each other as they ran towards the mountains to escape the flood. Soon the whole country was covered by water except for the tops of two mountains, which became the only islands in a wide, cold sea. Boris lived in one and Sam in the other.

It was cold. They liked snow, but it never snowed. Winter followed winter. The Giants forgot how lovely the summers used to be. Each day was just dull and terribly cold.

They grew more angry than ever, and instead of stones they now threw huge rocks at each other. On Mondays Sam would throw a rock at Boris. On Tuesdays

Boris would throw a rock at Sam. On Wednesdays it was Sam's turn to throw again, and so on, every day except Sundays, every week.

After both Giants had been struck many times on the ear and nose and the tops of their heads, their anger knew no limits.

The sea was dotted with rocks which the Giants had thrown, and one day Sam decided to use these rocks as giant stepping-stones. He waited until Boris was asleep, then picked up his huge stone club and climbed out of his mountain. He planned to reach the other island, hit Boris on the head, and make him sleep all day and miss his turn to throw a rock.

Sam leapt on to the first rock. Then he leapt on to the second rock.

As Sam reached the third rock, Boris opened one giant eye. He saw Sam, snatched his club and, whirling it round his head, jumped out of his mountain and began leaping from rock to rock towards his enemy. The whole world shook as the two Giants charged towards each other.

Suddenly both Giants stopped. Sam looked at the feet of Boris. Boris looked at the feet of Sam. Each Giant had one black-and-white sock and one red-and-blue sock. They stared at their odd socks for a long time.

Gradually they remembered the day the sea had covered the land. In their haste to escape the flood, the Giants had got their socks mixed. Now they could not even remember what they had been fighting about. They could only recall the years they had been friends.

They dropped their clubs into the sea, and laughed and danced.

When they returned to their islands, each found a small white flower and felt the sun warm on his shoulders. The sea began to recede. Flowers grew where the water had been. The birds returned to the

islands. Soon the two mountains were separated by nothing but a valley of trees. The country was large and beautiful once more.

Sam and Boris sat among the flowers, and sometimes a grasshopper would jump on to Sam's ear, or a butterfly would land on Boris's nose and birds would sit on the tops of their heads amidst the hair and flowers. The Giants were happy. The seasons came and went as before. Sometimes the Giants strode about their country, deep with grass or leaves or snow. Sometimes they made Giant footprints in the sand by the sea. Sometimes they

just lay in the woods which were full of birds and mari-
golds.

Whatever they did, they always wore odd socks. Even
when one of them had a new pair, he always gave one
sock to the Other Giant – just in case!

The Birds' Concert

ONE morning when Bobby Brewster woke up he felt
rather peculiar. First he shivered, and then he was far
too hot and started to cough. When his mother heard
him she came into his bedroom, had one look at his
flushed face, and took his temperature. It was 102.

'Just you stay in bed and I'm going to send for the
doctor,' she said. So she did.

Dr Hopkins is a fat and jolly man and he came later
in the morning. He looked at Bobby's throat, and
tapped his chest, and made him say 'Ah'. 'Have you got
a tummy ache?' he asked.

'I'm afraid I have,' said Bobby Brewster.

'Keep him in bed for a day or two. No rich food –
like sardines – And send round to the chemist for this
medicine.'

So they did. And when Bobby took his first dose of
medicine it tasted horrid.

He stayed in bed for two days, and by the next evening he felt a little better. Then, after he had been
tucked in but before it was dark, he was lying listening
to the birds saying, 'Good evening', to each other, when
a very funny thing happened. There was a tap-tap-tap
on the windowsill. Bobby turned over, and there,
standing on the windowsill, was a little bird. As soon
as it saw that Bobby was looking, it winked – a great big
wink with the left eye.

Of course Bobby winked back.

'Twitz – my friends in the winkers' club have asked me to fly up and see how you are – twitz,' said the bird.

'I'm a little better, thank you,' said Bobby. 'But still not quite well enough to get up.'

'That's good – twitz –' said the bird. 'We hope you will soon be quite well – twitz-twitz –'

'Thank you,' said Bobby Brewster. 'But what exactly do you mean by twitz?'

'I'm very sorry – twitz –' said the bird. 'But I've got a nasty cough – twitz-twitz – and that's how birds cough – twitz –'

'Oh, dear, I *am* sorry,' said Bobby. 'Are you taking anything for it?'

'I tried a bit of worm this morning, but it doesn't seem to have done much good,' said the bird.

'Have you got a tummy ache?' asked Bobby.

'Yes, I'm afraid I have,' said the bird.

'Do you know, I think you must have the same thing

wrong with you as I have,' said Bobby. 'The doctor said, "No rich food", so I shouldn't have any more worm if I were you.'

'No, I don't intend to,' said the bird.

Then Bobby Brewster had an idea.

'Why don't you try some of my medicine?' he said. 'It's done me good so it might help you.'

'What's it like?' asked the bird.

'Horrid,' said Bobby. 'But it's worth it if it makes you feel better.'

'Very well. Thank you, I think I will,' said the bird.

The medicine bottle was on Bobby's bedside table. He dipped in his little finger, and then held it over to the window. The bird hopped over and pecked at the drop of medicine on the end of his finger.

'Twitz-twitz-twitz-twitz,' it said, and hopped up and down.

'Whatever's the matter?' cried Bobby.

'My word, you were quite right when you said the medicine was horrid,' said the bird. 'I've never tasted anything so nasty in my life – twitz – I *had* intended to sing you to sleep, but with this cough I should only sing out of tune and annoy you – twitz – If your medicine does me good I will come with my concert party tomorrow and give you a show. Would you like that?'

'It will be lovely,' said Bobby – and the bird flew off, but it can't have lived far away because before he went to sleep Bobby could still hear the poor little thing twitz-twitzing in the trees.

The next morning at about seven o'clock Bobby opened a sleepy eye. Then a very funny thing happened. There was a tap-tap-tap-tap-tap-tapping on the window. Not just a tap-tap-tap this time, but a long tap-tap-tap-tap-tap. Bobby looked over, and there, standing on the windowsill, were seven birds. Bobby's friend, five other little birds like him – and a large fat black crow.

'Good morning, how do you feel?' asked the bird.

'I don't really know yet. I'm only just awake,' said Bobby. 'How are you?'

'I'm MUCH better,' said the bird. 'May I introduce you to Percy's Perkies?'

'Percy's Perkies?' said Bobby.

'Yes. I forgot to tell you last night that my name is Percy,' said the bird. 'And these are my Perkies.'

'How do you do?' said Bobby, and the birds all bowed politely.

'Shall we start the show?' asked Percy.

'Whenever you like,' said Bobby Brewster.

Well – you never saw such a show as those birds performed on Bobby Brewster's windowsill that morning. They had lovely voices – all except the crow – and they started with a song that Percy had specially written. This is how it went. (Sung to the tune of Boccerini's minuet.)

> *Isn't it a pity Bobby's got a stomach ache?*
> *Isn't it a pity Bobby's got a stomach ache?*
> *Oh he felt so ill, he had to take a pill.*
> *Bobby Brewster's got a stomach ache.*
> *With fun – skawk-skawk-skwark.*
> *And chaff – skwawk-skwawk-skwak.*
> *We'll make – skawk-skwawk-skwawk.*
> *Him laugh – skawwk-skwak-skwawk.*
> *Sing a little song and he'll forget his stomach ache.*
> *Won't be very long before he's lost his stomach ache.*
> *With some fun and rhythm, that's the stuff to give*
> *   'em.*
> *Bobby Brewster's got no stomach ache.*

Of course, the little birds sung the words and the fat crow did the skwawks.

After that they did a clever little dance on one leg all together – all except the crow, that is. He tried to, but fell bonk on his back feather, which made Bobby laugh and he had to hide his face under the pillow to stop making too much noise.

But that wasn't all. After that they did a very clever juggling act with some peas that they must have pecked out of the pods in the garden. They threw them from beak to beak, and balanced them on their back feathers

– all except the fat crow, that is – and he got a pea stuck so hard on his beak that he couldn't open his mouth. This made Bobby laugh so loudly that tears came into his eyes, the birds flew away, and Mrs Brewster came running into the bedroom.

'Whatever's the matter?' she cried. Then she looked at him more closely. 'You look much better,' she said.

'I AM much better,' said Bobby Brewster. And when Dr Hopkins came later that morning he said that Bobby had made a remarkable recovery and the medicine must have done him a lot of good.

I suppose that's true in a way, because, after all, the medicine had cured Percy the bird as well. But I don't think Bobby would have got better quite so quickly if he hadn't seen the marvellous show given by Percy's Perkies on his windowsill that morning, do you?

Which all goes to show what a good thing it is to be a member of the winkers' club, doesn't it?

Little Lisa

ONCE upon a time there was a little girl whose name was Lisa. She lived with her father and mother in a little red house in Delecarlia, Sweden.

Little Lisa's mother made her a beautiful orange-coloured dress. With it she wore a red-striped apron, a little red hood and a blue scarf. Her father bought her a pair of red shoes and a most beautiful parasol to go with the dress.

How lovely Little Lisa looked with all her new things!

'I am the prettiest girl in all Sweden,' thought Little Lisa.

One day Lisa's mother said, 'Put on your pretty dress and your new shoes, for today you are going to visit your grandmother. I have baked this cake for her. Follow the main road straight through the forest and you will soon be there.' Little Lisa was delighted; she clapped her hands in joy, for wasn't she going, all alone, to visit her grandmother who lived far away in the big forest? She might even stay overnight with Granny who told such wonderful fairy tales!

So Lisa promised to be careful to follow the main road, and kissing her mother good-bye, with her basket on her arm, she started off.

It was cool and pleasant in the forest, and Little Lisa enjoyed listening to the songs of the birds. After she had been walking a while she saw some wild strawberries, growing by the roadside.

'How delicious! I am so thirsty,' said Little Lisa as she stooped to pick them. How wonderful they tasted as she ate and ate. On and on she went; the farther she went, the bigger and the redder were the strawberries. Soon she was deep in the woods. Too late she remembered that she had promised her mother not to leave the road.

'Whatever shall I do?' cried the frightened little girl.

Just then she heard a deep growl, and looking up, saw a great big bear walking towards her.

'Grr! Grr! I am going to eat you,' said the bear.

'Oh, please don't, dear Uncle Bear,' begged Little Lisa. 'I will gladly give you my beautiful red-striped apron and my blue scarf if you will only let me go.'

'Very well,' said the bear. 'If you will give me your apron and your blue scarf, I won't eat you.'

So Little Lisa gave the big bear her red-striped apron and her blue scarf, and the bear trundled along, singing to himself, 'Now I am the prettiest bear in the whole forest.' Poor Little Lisa. Her tears fell fast. And there were so many trees she didn't know which way to turn!

All of a sudden she heard a terrible howl, and there, right in front of her, stood a big wolf, smacking his lips greedily.

'Ha! Ha! I am going to eat you,' said the wolf.

'Please, oh, please don't, dear Uncle Grey,' said Little Lisa. 'I will give you my beautiful orange dress if you will only let me go.'

'But the dress is too small for me,' answered the wolf.

'Perhaps you can use it for a head-dress,' said Little Lisa.

'That is not a bad idea,' said the wolf, as he put it on his head; and walking proudly away, he said to himself, 'Now I am the most beautiful wolf in the whole big forest.'

Little Lisa continued on her way. 'If I can only find my way home, I won't mind,' she sighed.

But once again she heard a strange noise. This time it was a big red fox that stood right in front of her.

'Aha! What a fine meal! Don't move, for I am going to eat you,' said the fox.

'No, please don't, dear Mr Fox,' said Little Lisa. 'I will gladly give you my beautiful blue parasol if you will only let me go.'

'Well,' said the fox, 'that is a pretty blue parasol. Give it to me and I will let you go.'

So Little Lisa gave him her beautiful blue parasol and Mr Fox ran happily away, saying to himself:

'I am now the finest fox in the whole big forest.'

Poor Little Lisa, how she cried! All she had left were the little red hood, and her pretty red shoes. She had given away all her other things. She had even lost

her basket! She must have forgotten to pick it up when the bear frightened her. As the shadows grew darker and darker in the big black forest, she tried hard to be brave and to keep on walking. The stars twinkled brightly in the black sky while the Old Man in the Moon smiled kindly down on her. Tired out, she sat down on a big stone to rest. She thought of all the beautiful clothes she had had to give away; she thought of her mother at home in the cosy cottage; she thought of her grandmother, watching and waiting for her to come. And there she was, lost in the great big forest. Poor Little Lisa! How she cried!

Suddenly, she heard a little voice near her say, 'Why are you crying, little girl?'

There, close to her feet, sat a little rabbit.

'If you don't answer me,' said the rabbit, flapping his long pink ears, 'I must run away, for I am in a hurry. Ha! What nice shoes you have. Would you give them to me to help me run faster?'

'Take them, take them, dear Mr Bunny,' said Little Lisa. 'All my other beautiful clothes are now gone, so I won't need the shoes. Take them and put them on your hind feet.' And she gave Mr Bunny her pretty red shoes.

'Many thanks,' said the rabbit, as he put on the red shoes. 'You are certainly a very nice little girl. And because you are such a good little girl, you may get up on my back, and you will see how fast we can travel.'

So Little Lisa climbed up on his back, and away they went like the wind. You can be sure Little Lisa held on tight. She didn't want to fall off.

As they galloped happily along, the silence of the deep forest was broken by a terrible noise.

'Oh!' cried Little Lisa. 'I think that must be the bear, the wolf and the fox, who are coming to eat me up. Hurry, hurry.'

'Don't be afraid, Little Lisa,' said the rabbit. 'If you hold on tight, nobody can catch us. I can run faster than anyone in the whole forest. But first let's look and make sure just what it is all about,' said the rabbit. So saying, they hid behind a big tree.

Little Lisa peeped out and what do you think she saw? There stood the bear, the wolf and the fox, quarrelling as to which of them was the most beautiful animal in the whole forest. Furiously and loudly they argued. In their anger they tore off their clothes in order to be better able to fight.

Mr Fox, who was very clever, started to run round and round a big tree. Mr Bear and Mr Wolf followed. Mr Bear grabbed hold of Mr Fox's tail and Mr Fox took hold of Mr Wolf's tail; Mr Wolf, in turn, took hold of Mr Bear's little, short tail, and so round and round, and faster and faster went the three!

But while they were chasing one another in this way, Little Lisa sneaked up and grabbed all her clothes. 'If you don't want my beautiful clothes, I might as well take them back,' she said. But the bear, the wolf, and the fox were too busy growling at each other to notice her. They became more and more angry. 'Brr, brr! Grr, grr! Growl, growl!' Faster and faster they ran. They ran so fast that Little Lisa could hardly see them. They had no time to look around. Quickly Little Lisa put on her clothes, and, taking her parasol, ran to Mr Bunny, who was waiting for her behind the tree.

'I think we'd better hurry away before they see us,' said Little Lisa, as she climbed up on the back of Mr Bunny.

'If you run straight home to Mother and Father, I will give you some hot waffles with jam,' said she coaxingly.

'That sounds good to me,' said Mr Bunny, running faster than ever.

It wasn't long before they arrived home. You can imagine how surprised Little Lisa's mother was when she caught sight of her little daughter, riding on Mr Bunny's back. And she was even more surprised when Little Lisa told her all that had happened to her in the big forest.

'You see what happens, when you don't obey? You shouldn't have left the main road, Little Lisa,' said her mother. But because she was so happy to have her home again, she forgave her and said: 'Let's have a party to celebrate your safe return, and since you have promised Mr Bunny waffles and jam I think we might make it a real waffle party.'

And so she lighted the stove and soon the smell of delicious waffles filled the house. She made piles and piles of them and when they were ready, Little Lisa and Father and Mother and the friendly little Mr Bunny sat down to supper. How wonderful they tasted and how they ate and ate!

To tell the truth, Mr Bunny ate fifty-nine waffles; Lisa's mother ate seventy; her father eighty-two and, as for Little Lisa, she was so very, very hungry that she ate one hundred and thirty-three waffles.

Can you believe it?

How the Engine Learned the Knowing Song

ONCE there was a new engine. He had a great big boiler; he had a smoke stack; he had a bell; he had a whistle; he had a sand-dome; he had a headlight; he had four big driving wheels; he had a cab. But he was very sad, was this engine, for he didn't know how to use any of his parts. All around him on the tracks were other engines, puffing or whistling or ringing their bells and squirting steam. One big engine moved his wheels slowly, softly muttering to himself, 'I'm going, I'm going, I'm going.' Now the new engine knew this was the end of the Knowing Song of Engines. He wanted desperately to sing it. So he called out:

> *'I want to go*
> *But I don't know how;*
> *I want to know,*
> *Please teach me now.*
> *Please somebody teach me how.'*

Now there were two men who had come just on purpose to teach him how. And who do you suppose they were? The engineer and the fireman! When the engineer heard the new engine call out, he asked, 'What do you want, new engine?' And the engine answered:

How the Engine Learned the Knowing Song

'*I want the sound*
Of my wheels going round.
I want to stream
A jet of steam.
I want to puff
Smoke and stuff.
I want to ring
Ding, ding-a-ding.
I want to blow
My whistle so.
I want my light
To shine bright.
I want to go ringing and singing the song.
The humming song of the engine coming,
The clear, near song of the engine here,
The knowing song of the engine going.'

Now the engineer and the fireman were pleased when they heard what the new engine wanted. But the engineer said:

'*All in good time, my engine,*
Steady, steady.
'*Til you're ready.*
Learn to know
Before you go.'

Then he said to the fireman, 'First we must give our engine some water.' So they put the end of a hose hanging from a big high-up tank right into a little tank under the engine's tender. The water filled up this little tank and then ran into the big boiler and filled that all up too. And while they were doing this the water kept saying:

> *'I am water from a stream*
> *When I'm hot I turn to steam.'*

When the engine felt his boiler full of water he asked eagerly:

> *'Now I have water,*
> *Now do I know*
> *How I should go?'*

But the fireman said:

> *'All in good time, my engine,*
> *Steady, steady,*
> *'Till you're ready.*
> *Learn to know*
> *Before you go.'*

Then he said to the engineer, 'Now we must give our engine some coal.' So they filled the tender with coal, and then under the boiler the fireman built a fire. Then the fireman began blowing and the coals began glowing. And as he built the fire, the fire said:

> *'I am fire,*
> *The coal I eat*
> *To make the heat*
> *To turn the stream*
> *Into the steam.'*

When the engine felt the sleeping fire wake up and begin to live inside him and turn the water into steam he said eagerly:

How the Engine Learned the Knowing Song

> *'Now I have water,*
> *Now I have coal,*
> *Now do I know*
> *How I should go?'*

But the engineer said:

> *'All in good time, my engine,*
> *Steady, steady,*
> *'Til you're ready.*
> *Learn to know*
> *Before you go.'*

Then he said to the fireman, 'We must oil our engine well.' So they took oil cans with funny long noses and they oiled all the machinery, the piston-rods, the levers, the wheels, everything that moved or went round. And all the time the oil kept saying:

> *'No creak,*
> *No squeak.'*

When the engine felt the oil smoothing all his machinery, he said eagerly:

> *'Now I have water,*
> *Now I have coal,*
> *Now I am oiled,*
> *Now do I know*
> *How I should go?*

But the fireman said:

> '*All in good time, my engine,*
> *Steady, steady,*
> *Till you're ready.*
> *Learn to know*
> *Before you go.*'

Then he said to the engineer, 'We must give our engine some sand.' So they took some sand and they filled the sand domes on top of the boiler so that he could send sand down through his two little pipes and sprinkle it in front of his wheels when the rails were slippery. And all the time the sand kept saying:

> '*When ice drips,*
> *And wheel slips,*
> *I am sand*
> *Close at hand.*'

When the new engine felt his sand dome filled with sand he said eagerly:

> '*Now I have water,*
> *Now I have coal,*
> *Now I am oiled,*
> *Now I have sand,*
> *Now do I know*
> *How I should go?*'

But the engineer said:

> '*All in good time, my engine,*
> *Steady, steady,*
> '*Til you're ready.*
> *Learn to know*
> *Before you go.*'

Then he said to the fireman, 'We must light our engine's headlight.' So the fireman took a cloth and he wiped the curved mirror behind the light and polished the brass around it. Then he screwed in a big electric bulb and closed the little door in front of it. And then he turned a switch. All the time the light kept saying:

> *'I'm the headlight shining bright
> Like a sunbeam through the night.'*

Now when the engine saw the great golden path of brightness streaming out ahead of him, he said eagerly:

> *'Now I have water
> Now I have coal,
> Now I am oiled,
> Now I have sand,
> Now I make light,
> Now do I know
> How I should go?'*

And the engineer said, 'We will see if you are ready, my new engine.' So he climbed into the cab and the fireman got in behind him. Then he said, 'Engine, can you blow your whistle so?' And he pulled a handle which let the steam into the whistle and the engine whistled 'Toot, toot, toot.' Then he said, 'Can you puff smoke and stuff?' And the engine puffed black smoke saying, 'Puff, puff, puff, puff, puff.' Then he said, 'Engine, can you squirt a stream of steam?' And he opened a valve and the engine went, 'Szszszszsz.' Then he said, 'Engine, can you sprinkle sand?' And he pulled a little handle and the sand trickled drip,

drip, drip, drip down on the tracks in front of the engine's wheels. Then he said, 'Engine, does your light shine out bright?' And he looked and there was a great golden flood of light on the track in front of him. Then he said, 'Engine, can you make the sound of your wheels going round?' And he pulled another lever and

the great wheels began to move. Then the engineer said:

> 'Now is the time,
> Now is the time.
> Steady, steady,
> Now you're ready.

'Blow whistle, ring bell, puff smoke, hiss steam, sprinkle sand, shine light, turn wheels!

> ''Tis time to be ringing and singing the song,
> The humming song of the engine coming,

How the Engine Learned the Knowing Song

The clear, near song of the engine here,
The knowing song of the engine going.'

Then whistle blew, bell rang, smoke puffed, steam hissed, sand sprinkled, light shone and wheels turned like this:

'Toot-toot, ding-a-ding, puff-puff,
Szszszszsz, drip-drip, chug-chug.'

That's the way the new engine sounded when he started on his first ride and didn't know how to do things very well. But that's not the way he sounded when he had learned to go really smooth and fast. Then it was that he learned *really* to sing 'The Knowing Song of the Engine'. He sang it better than anyone else for he became the fastest, the steadiest, the most knowing of all express engines. And this is the song he sang. You could hear it humming on the rails long before he came and hear it humming on the rails long after he had passed. Now listen to the song.

'I'm coming, I'm coming, I'm coming, I'm coming,
I'm coming, I'm coming, I'm coming, I'm coming,
I'm coming, I'm coming, I'm coming, I'm coming,
I'm Coming, I'm Coming, I'm Coming, I'm Coming,
I'M HERE, I'M HERE, I'M HERE, I'M HERE,
I'M HERE, I'M HERE, I'M HERE, I'M HERE.
I'm Going, I'm Going, I'm Going, I'm Going,
I'm going, I'm going, I'm going, I'm going,
I'm going, I'm going, I'm going, I'm going.'

The Little Rooster
and the Diamond Button

SOMEWHERE, at some place beyond the Seven Seas, there lived a poor old woman. The poor old woman had a Little Rooster. One day the Little Rooster walked out of the yard to look for strange insects and worms. All the insects and worms in the yard were his friends – he was hungry, but he could not eat his friends! So he walked out to the road. He scratched and he scratched. He scratched out a Diamond Button. Of all things, a Diamond Button! The Button twinkled at him. 'Pick me up, Little Rooster, take me to your old mistress. She likes Diamond Buttons.'

'Cock-a-doodle-doo. I'll pick you up and take you to my poor old mistress!'

So he picked up the Button. Just then the Turkish Sultan walked by. The Turkish Sultan was very, very fat. Three fat servants walked behind him, carrying the wide, wide bag of the Turkish Sultan's trousers. He saw the Little Rooster with the Diamond Button.

'Little Rooster, give me your Diamond Button.'

'No, indeed, I won't. I am going to give it to my poor old mistress. She likes Diamond Buttons.'

But the Turkish Sultan liked Diamond Buttons, too. Besides, he could not take 'no' for an answer. He turned to his three fat servants.

'Catch the Little Rooster and take the Diamond Button from him.'

The three fat servants dropped the wide, wide bag of the Turkish Sultan's trousers, caught the Little Rooster, and took the Diamond Button away from him. The Turkish Sultan took the Diamond Button home with him and put it in his treasure chamber.

The Little Rooster was very angry. He went to the palace of the Turkish Sultan, perched on the window, and cried:

'Cock-a-doodle-doo! Turkish Sultan, give me back my Diamond Button.'

The Turkish Sultan did not like this, so he walked into another room.

The Little Rooster perched on the window of another room and cried: 'Cock-a-doodle-doo! Turkish Sultan, give me back my Diamond Button.'

The Turkish Sultan was mad. He called his three fat servants.

'Catch the Little Rooster. Throw him into the well, let him drown!'

The three fat servants caught the Little Rooster and threw him into the well. But the Little Rooster cried: 'Come, my empty stomach, come, my empty stomach, drink up all the water.'

His empty stomach drank up all the water.

The Little Rooster flew back to the window and cried: 'Cock-a-doodle-doo! Turkish Sultan, give me back my Diamond Button.'

The Turkish Sultan was madder than before. He called his three fat servants.

'Catch the Little Rooster and throw him into the fire. Let him burn!'

The three fat servants caught the Little Rooster and threw him into the fire.

But the Little Rooster cried: 'Come, my full stomach, let out all the water to put out all the fire.'

His full stomach let out all the water. It put out all the fire.

He flew back to the window again and cried: 'Cock-a-doodle-doo! Turkish Sultan, give me back my Diamond Button.'

The Turkish Sultan was madder than ever. He called his three fat servants.

'Catch the Little Rooster, throw him into a beehive, and let the bees sting him!'

The three fat servants caught the Little Rooster and threw him into a beehive. But the Little Rooster cried: 'Come, my empty stomach, come, my empty stomach, eat up all the bees.'

His empty stomach ate up all the bees.

He flew back to the window again and cried: 'Cock-a-doodle-doo! Turkish Sultan, give me back my Diamond Button.'

The Turkish Sultan was so mad he didn't know what to do. He called his three fat servants.

'What shall I do with the Little Rooster?'

The first fat servant said: 'Hang him on the flag-pole!'

The second fat servant said: 'Cut his head off!'

The third fat servant said: '*Sit* on him!'

The Turkish Sultan cried: 'That's it! I'll sit on him! Catch the Little Rooster and bring him to me!'

The three fat servants caught the Little Rooster and brought him to the Turkish Sultan. The Turkish Sultan opened the wide, wide bag of his trousers and put the Little Rooster in. Then he sat on him.

But the Little Rooster cried, 'Come, my full stomach, let out all the bees to sting the Turkish Sultan.'

His stomach let out all the bees.

And did they sting the Turkish Sultan?

THEY DID!

The Turkish Sultan jumped up in the air.

'Ouch! Ouch! Ow! Ow!' he cried. 'Take this Little Rooster to my treasure chamber and let him find his confounded Diamond Button!'

The three fat servants took the Little Rooster to the treasure chamber.

'Find your confounded Diamond Button!' they said and left him.

But the Little Rooster cried: 'Come, my empty stomach, come, my empty stomach, eat up all the money.'

His empty stomach ate up all the money in the Turkish Sultan's treasure chamber.

Then the Little Rooster waddled home as fast as he could and gave all the money to his poor old mistress. Then he went out into the yard to tell his friends, the insects and worms, about the Turkish Sultan and the Diamond Button.

Little Laura
and the Lonely Ostrich

LITTLE LAURA was very excited because she was going to the Zoo, with her Nannie and her best friend, Billie Guftie.

The turnstiles went click! click! as they entered the main gates.

'Have we anything to feed the animals with?' asked Billie Guftie.

'I have a bun in my pocket,' said Laura.

They went first to see the elephants, a mother elephant and a baby elephant. Laura offered her bun. But the mother elephant's trunk swished about making snuffling noises.

'I ... I don't care for it,' said Laura, drawing back. Billie Guftie helped her hold the bun steady. The mother elephant took it, and curling her trunk round put it into her mouth.

'Look at the baby elephant. Isn't he sweet?' said Nannie. But that naughty baby filled his trunk with water and squirted a bystander. 'I hope he's not going to squirt us,' said Laura and ran away from that mischievous beast.

They came to a signpost which said TO THE LLAMA ARBOUR.

'What is a llama?' asked Laura.

'Let's go and see,' said Nannie.

Outside the Arbour was a notice saying, 'Llama, a woolly ruminant from the South.' Inside was a lordly llama harnessed to a little painted carriage.

'What a haughty expression he has,' said Laura.

But a keeper told her that his face was just made that way. 'He's not *very* haughty,' he said. 'Would you like to ride in his carriage?'

'Yes, please,' said Laura.

So she and Billie Guftie scrambled into a little painted carriage. They proceeded slowly out of the Arbour and down the avenue in a sedate manner.

'This is not much fun,' remarked Billie Guftie. 'Can't we go faster?'

The llama turned and gave him a long cool stare as if to say, 'How dare you criticize my stately ways?'

He then sat down in the avenue and absolutely refused to move. Nothing the keeper could do would persuade him to get up. 'I hope I'm not going to weep,' said Little Laura. But just then a cheerful voice was heard ...

... It was Grebo! Grebo the Special! The Most Special of all Special Policemen. Grebo often came to the Zoo to inspect the animals and make sure they were happy. He was leading Orly Ostrich. This unhappy bird was grieving and pining for his wife, who was left behind at his home in the Sunshine Island.

Grebo suggested that Orly should pull the painted carriage. 'It would cheer him up,' he said.

'Goodness gracious me!' cried Nannie. She feared

a bird might be rather flighty. But Grebo said, 'Let us *all* go for a ride. I would love to come too!'

'That would be delightful, Grebo,' said Nannie. So Orly was harnessed to the painted carriage, while the llama looked on with cool indifference.

Orly trotted off at a merry pace for a joy-ride round the Zoo. 'What larkish fun!' cried Little Laura, as they tripped along looking at all the strange and wonderful

creatures. But soon Orly started going very fast indeed. Laura was rather alarmed. Even the animals in their cages were surprised to see a bird going so swiftly. 'Whoa! Whoa!' cried Grebo, but Orly took no notice. Faster! Faster! Now Orly was really racing along, with wings outstretched and face well forward. A small crowd gasped, 'My! That ostrich is going a pace!'

When they reached the parapet at the end of the Zoo, to everyone's horrified amazement, Orly spread out his wings and flew into the air. 'Hold on to your moufflon

hat, Laura!' cried Nannie, as they swept over the
parapet ... over the Great City ...

'Go back!' called Grebo sternly, but Orly did not
appear to hear him. They grasped the sides of the little
painted carriage and gazed about in fear.

When they reached the open country Grebo said,
'Don't worry. Orly will get tired soon. Then he will
have to come down and we can take the bus home.'

'Meanwhile,' said Nannie, 'we will enjoy ourselves
looking at the scenery.'

Suddenly Billie Guftie shouted, 'Look! The sea!
The sea!' Soon they were flying over the tall cliffs with
waves crashing far below. Laura was frightened. But
Nannie said, 'What must be must be,' and everyone
was comforted.

On and on they flew over the deep dark sea. Orly
began to look tired and flapped his wings wearily.
Nannie was secretly very alarmed. Suddenly Grebo
shouted, 'Land Ahoy!' and far away they saw a beautiful desert island. As they got nearer they felt sure it
must be the Sunshine Island for there, gazing wistfully
out to sea, was a lovely little ostrich ... Orly's wife!

By now Orly was very tired indeed and flapped his
wings feebly. Grebo feared he would never make land.
But when he saw his lovely wife he made a tremendous
effort ... and landed with a crash at her feet. In doing
so his harness came undone and everyone was flung on
to the beach. The little painted carriage was swept out
to sea and disappeared over the horizon. 'Well, that's
that,' said Nannie. 'We're shipwrecked.'

They sat dismally on the shore. The situation was

very grave, and Laura was getting hungry. Only Orly and his wife were happy, chatting together with their wings round each other. Suddenly they heard strange noises and loud shrieks. Orly and his wife jumped up and scampered over the rocks, towards the jungly hills from where the noise was coming. Grebo followed swiftly. 'Could it be savages!' he wondered fearfully. 'Take care!' called Nannie, as Laura and Billie Guftie started scrambling after him.

They soon found the cause of the commotion.

Among the palms and tropical plants, a group of ostriches were greeting Orly and his wife with welcoming screeches.

'They must be Orly's cousins,' said Grebo.

Just then they heard Nannie calling urgently.

They looked down and saw her waving to a magnificent white yacht sailing by.

'Why! It's the Royal Yacht!' exclaimed Grebo.

'It's not stopping,' cried Billie Guftie in dismay.

The King and his bodyguard, Sir Archie Argyle, were strolling about the deck. The King was singing. He sang so loudly that neither he nor Sir Archie Argyle could hear Nannie's shouts.

> *'Oh! What a wondrous thing!*
> *To be a Royal King!*
> *To have my yacht ...*
> *Right on this spot!*
> *Ho, ho, ho, ho! Ha, ha, ha, ha!'*

Grebo and the children yelled and shouted as they ran towards the shore. But still the yacht sailed on.

Grebo feared they would be stranded on the island for ever. Now Orly and his cousins joined in with shrieks so loud and piercing that the King at last heard the noise and stopped singing.

'Are you shipwrecked?' he called.

'Yes. We are.'

'Would you like me take you home in my yacht?'

'Yes, PLEASE.'

The King turned to Sir Archie Argyle. 'Tell the crew we'll stop here,' he said. The yacht was brought alongside the rocks and a gangway was put down.

'Please step aboard, my friends!' cried the King. 'And welcome to my yacht.'

He greeted his guests on the deck. Nannie loved Royalty. 'Your Majesty! Your Majesty!' she murmured, as he shook her by the hand. 'You must be famished,' he said.

Some more guests now appeared on the gangway and walked noisily up ... Orly and his wife and cousins!

'They must want to come and live in the Zoo,' said Laura. The King was a bit surprised, but welcomed the ostriches cordially.

He then invited all his guests into the State Cabin, where an elegant feast was laid out. 'I always have plenty of food on the table,' he said, 'in case some shipwrecked people come on board.'

Laura was very fond of eating, so she enjoyed herself immensely. By the time the feast was over, the moon had come out, the stars were shining and the Royal Yacht was speeding home. Laura and her friends

strolled on the deck in the moonlight. Orly looked happy because he knew he would never be lonely again. For now not only would he have his lovely wife with him at the Zoo, but all his cousins as well.

The Sun and the Wind

THE Wind had been blowing hard all morning and was feeling particularly pleased with himself.

He looked at the Sun who was beaming splendidly above the hilltops.

'I'm stronger than you,' said the Wind to the Sun.

'No, you are not,' smiled the Sun back at him.

'Yes, I am.'

'No, you're not.'

'Yes, I am.'

'No, you're not.'

'Very well then,' said the Wind. 'Do you see that man down there, wearing a coat? Let's see which of us is powerful enough to make him take it off.'

'I agree,' said the Sun.

So the Wind began to blow. He puffed and puffed for all he was worth and the man's coat began blowing about crazily all over the place. But the more the Wind blew the more the man clung tightly to his coat and wrapped it closely round him. He would *not* let it blow away and so the Wind could not get it off.

'Now it's my turn,' smiled the Sun.

He shone his sunny beams all over the man's face and body. The man began to feel warmer and warmer. He unbuttoned his coat. The Sun's rays beat down upon the man until he felt uncomfortably hot. He took off his coat and sat down.

'I've won,' said the Sun.

Tom Thumb

HAVE you heard of King Arthur and the Knights of the Round Table? Well, in his palace there was a famous magician named Merlin who used to travel around the countryside disguised as an old beggar, helping poor people and trying to make them happy.

One day Merlin stopped at a farmer's cottage. The farmer and his wife invited him in and offered him food and shelter. Merlin was so struck by their kind hospitality that he wanted to do something very special for them.

'What do you need most?' he asked the farmer. The farmer was puzzled by this question from the poor beggar (remember, Merlin was disguised), but he said:

'Have you noticed how sad my poor wife is? We have lived here for ten long years and we have no child.'

'Yes,' continued the farmer's wife sadly, 'I would dearly love to have a son of my own. I shouldn't mind how small he was – even if he were no bigger than my husband's thumb.'

Merlin nodded, thanked them for their kindness and left.

Shortly afterwards the good farmer's wife had a son and a strong bonny baby he was; he was very clever and full of tricks. But he never grew any taller than his father's thumb and so they called him Tom Thumb. One day, when his mother was stirring the batter for a pudding, Tom climbed up on to the edge of the bowl to see what was happening. He slipped and – splosh! in he fell. His mother was so busy stirring, she didn't notice. She poured the batter into the pan ready for cooking. Tom's tiny mouth was so full that he couldn't scream but he kicked so lustily that his mother thought the pudding was bewitched, so she threw the whole thing outside.

A tinker passing the cottage door picked it up and put it in his bundle. By now Tom had spat most of the batter out of his mouth and bawled for all his tiny lungs were worth. The tinker was so scared that he threw the bowl away and Tom struggled free and crept home, all covered with sticky batter.

His mother was delighted to have him home again. She washed him clean in a teacup of water and put him to bed.

Next day his mother took him to the meadow when she went to milk the cow. As it was rather windy she tied Tom to a thistle to stop him from being blown away while she did the milking. But the cow caught sight of the thistle with its oak leaf hat and took it all in one big mouthful with poor Tom inside. Tom was so scared of the cow's big teeth that he shouted loudly:

'Mother, Mother! I'm inside the cow's mouth. Get me out!'

His mother rushed up to the cow, which was so surprised by the odd noises inside her mouth that she dropped him out and Tom's mother caught him neatly in her apron. Then she took him home, gave him his supper and put him to bed.

Next day, when Tom ran out in the fields with his father he fell into a tiny ditch and before his father could find him, a raven swooped down low and carried him aloft in its beak. Higher and higher it flew and Tom was so scared that he kicked and kicked for all he

was worth – for he was quite strong despite his tiny size. The raven opened its beak to get a firmer grip, but Tom slipped and fell – right down into a great river, where he was immediately gobbled up by a big fish.

A fisherman had his net out just at that spot and caught the fish. The fish was taken to the market and was bought by the King's Own Angler-in-Chief, who took it to King Arthur's palace for the royal dinner. Imagine the Royal Cook's surprise when she cut the fish open and found Tom Thumb inside – alive and well, though a bit frightened. All the scullions and kitchen-maids gathered round to have a peep at him. The cook took him to King Arthur himself and Tom bowed low as he was set down on the King's Round Table. The knights and their ladies laughed and clapped but Merlin, the Royal Magician (who, of course, knew where Tom had come from), only smiled quietly.

After he had stayed at the Court for a few days amusing everyone with his mischievous tricks, King Arthur summoned him and asked:

'Tell me, Tom, how big are your mother and father? Are they little folk like yourself?'

'No, Your Majesty,' said Tom, 'my father is as tall as the next man and my mother is not a little woman either. They are poor folk and work hard in the fields all day long.'

King Arthur then led Tom to his Treasury, where all his gold and silver was kept.

'Look, Tom,' he said, 'take as much of this as you can back home to your parents.' Tom picked up a golden sovereign which was nearly as big as himself and hoisted it on to his back. King Arthur smiled. 'You have chosen well,' he said. 'This will keep your parents well provided for many years.'

So Tom set off home with the sovereign on his back and after two whole days and many rests he reached his father's cottage.

How delighted his mother and father were to see him: how proud they were to receive King Arthur's golden sovereign. But poor Tom was so utterly weary after his long journey that he had to rest in bed for many days.

When he felt his old self again, he told his mother and father that he must go back to King Arthur's court. Reluctantly they let him go.

The King was so overjoyed to see him again that he decided to make him a knight.

A special meeting of the King's Tailors was called to measure Tom for his very special clothes. They decided to make his coat and cloak of royal purple velvet and his breeches of the softest calf's hide and his hose of gossamer silk. The Royal Bootmaker cut his boots out of the finest goatskin. Then before the assembled court he rode in a tiny glass coach drawn by four white mice.

King Arthur also had a special tiny gold palace built for him.

But for all these honours, Tom never forgot his parents and every so often he would ride off in his coach to visit them.

So the poor farmer and his wife were proud of their little son, but they never realized that all this had happened through the magic of the disguised old beggar who had called at their cottage many years ago.

The Lory who Longed
for Honey

ONCE upon a time, in a hot sunny country, lived a very
bright and beautiful parrot. He was red and green and
gold and blue, with a dark purple top to his head. His
real name was Lory. And he lived on honey.

There were hundreds of flowers growing among the
trees, so all he had to do when he was hungry was to fly
down and lick the honey out of the flowers. As a matter
of fact, he had a tongue that was specially shaped for
getting honey out of flowers. So he always had plenty to
eat, and managed very well. All day long he flew about
in the hot sunshine, while the monkeys chattered and
the bright birds screamed. And as long as he had plenty
of honey, he was perfectly happy.

Then one day a sailor came to the forest looking for
parrots. He found the parrot that liked honey and took
him away. He didn't know that this parrot's real name
was a Lory. He didn't know that he had a tongue
specially shaped for getting honey out of flowers. He
didn't even know he liked honey. He only knew he was
a very bright and beautiful parrot and he meant to take
him to England and sell him. So on board the ship he
fed the parrot on sunflower seeds and taught him to
say: 'What have you got, what have you got, what have
you got for me?' And whenever the Lory said this, the

sailor gave him a sunflower seed. Although, as a matter of fact, he would very much sooner have had honey.

When they reached England, the sailor sold the parrot who liked honey to an old lady who lived in a cottage on a hill. She didn't know much about parrots. She didn't know the parrot was a Lory. She didn't know he had a special tongue for licking honey out of flowers. She didn't even know he liked honey.

But she thought his red and green feathers, his gold and blue feathers, and the dark purple feathers on the top of his head were beautiful. She called him Polly, and fed him on bits of bread and biscuit.

Whenever he said, as he often did: 'What have you got, what have you got, what have you got for me?' she would give him a bit of bread or biscuit. But, of course, he would very much sooner have had honey.

Now the old lady lived by herself and had to work very hard to make enough money to buy food. Generally she had just bread and margarine for tea, because she couldn't afford to buy honey even for herself, although she liked it.

Then one day when she wasn't in the least expecting it, the old lady's nephew who lived in South Africa sent her a present. It was a wooden box carefully packed with straw. Some of the straw was already poking between the boards, but it was impossible to tell what was inside.

When the postman brought it, he said: 'Looks like a nice surprise, lady. Maybe some jam or some fruit.'

She carried the box carefully into her sitting-room and unfastened it. It wasn't jam or fruit. It was six jars of honey all wrapped up in straw. Inside was a note which said:

Dear Auntie,

I have managed to get a very nice job in South Africa, and I am making quite a bit of money. I am sure you are not able to buy all the things you need, so I am sending you six jars of honey. If you like them, I will send some more.

Love from your nephew – Robert

When she had read the letter she was tremendously excited and pleased, because it was so long since anyone had sent her a present and today it wasn't even her birthday. She took out the jars very carefully and put them in a row in the larder. Then she cleared up all the straw and paper and string, and said to herself: 'I'll start the first jar at tea-time today.'

When the clock struck half-past three, the old lady put the kettle on the gas, and began to cut some bread. It was certainly rather early for tea, but the old lady was so excited about the honey that she couldn't wait any longer. She put the bread and margarine on the table, took a plate and a knife, and a cup and saucer and spoon out of the cupboard, and then she went to the larder.

All this made Polly very excited. He wasn't in his cage, but on a separate perch where he could turn somersaults if he liked. The old lady let him sit here in the afternoons. He could tell it was tea-time, and when the old lady went to the larder he expected she would bring out some cake or fruit.

So he shouted at the top of his voice: 'What have you got, what have you got, what have you got for me?' When the old lady brought out neither cake nor fruit, but only a jar of yellow stuff, Polly was rather puzzled. But as soon as he saw her take some on her knife and spread the sticky stuff on her bread, and eat it with such pleasure, he knew it was honey.

And as soon as he knew it was honey, he knew he absolutely must think of some way of getting it for himself.

The old lady never dreamt of giving the Lory honey. She didn't know much about parrots. She didn't know he was called a Lory. She didn't know he had a tongue specially shaped for getting honey out of flowers. She didn't even know he liked honey.

But all the time the old lady was spreading the honey on her first slice of bread and thinking how wonderfully kind her nephew was to send it, and what an unexpected treat it was, the Lory was working out a plan.

Now parrots, as you know, are very clever at remembering words and also at imitating people, and sometimes when they talk they can make their voice sound as if it is coming from a different part of the house altogether, so that you have no idea it is the parrot talking at all.

While the old lady was eating her bread and honey and enjoying it tremendously, she suddenly heard a *Miaow!* It was really the Lory, but she didn't know that.

'There's a kitten outside,' she said. 'Poor thing, I expect it's lost. I'll let it in so that it can get warm by the fire.' And she went to the door and opened it.

Polly just had time to flutter on to the table and take a mouthful of honey with his special tongue and get on his perch again before she came back.

'How very strange,' she said, 'I'm sure I heard a kitten. Yet I've looked in the street, and there isn't a kitten to be seen.'

Polly winked and shouted: 'What have you got, what have you got, what have you got for me?' But the old lady still didn't know he was after the honey.

While the lady was spreading her *second* slice of bread, he thought of another plan. This time he made a noise like the kettle boiling over.

'Goodness!' cried the old lady, jumping up. 'That will put the stove out, unless I hurry.'

And while she rushed out into the kitchen, Polly flew down and took his second big mouthful of honey.

'That's very peculiar,' said the old lady, coming back again just as Polly scrambled on to his perch. 'The kettle's perfectly all right, and not boiling over at all.' But she still didn't understand the Lory was after her honey.

Then he had what he thought was his best plan of all. He made a noise like big drops of rain falling on the roof.

'Oh heavens!' said the poor old lady. 'Now I shall have to bring all the washing in.'

And she left her tea with the pot of honey standing on the table, and went outside to fetch in the washing before it got soaked.

She was a long time, because she had washed a table-cloth, two sheets, a pillow-slip, a towel, a frock, a cardigan and the curtains from the sitting-room. And while she was taking them off the line, the Lory was swallowing honey as fast as he could.

At last, her arms full of washing, the old lady came back into the room. 'That's funny,' she said, as she looked at the window. 'The sun is shining as brightly as ever. I do believe I've brought all the washing in for nothing.'

'And that's funnier still!' she went on with a little scream, looking at the table. 'I do believe someone's been eating my honey!'

She picked up the jar and looked at it. There was just a scraping left at the bottom. Yet she had only opened the jar a few minutes ago.

'It must be a burglar,' she said, and feeling very brave she began to look under the furniture and inside the cupboards and wherever a burglar might find space to hide.

All the time she was hunting, the Lory was turning somersaults on his perch and shrieking at the top of his voice: 'What have you got, what have you got, what have you got for me?' He felt very pleased with himself, and he didn't care a bit that he had made the old lady go to all the trouble of bringing in her washing, and on top of that had eaten almost the whole of a jar of honey that her nephew had sent from South Africa.

When the old lady had decided there was no burglar in the house, she went back to the tea-table. And then she noticed drips of honey leading over the table-cloth, over the floor, and up to Polly's perch. She reached up and touched his perch, and sure enough, that was sticky too.

'Why, you rascal!' she said. 'I do believe it was you who stole the honey.'

And that was how the old lady who didn't know much about parrots discovered that Lories like honey better than anything else in the world. After that, she always gave her Lory some honey for his tea, and she managed it quite well because her nephew in South Africa sent her six jars every month.

But do you know, she never found out it was the Lory who played those tricks on her just to get a taste of her honey!

All Change!

THERE were once four friends. They were a small ginger kitten, a small white puppy, a little brown rabbit and a baby rook. They lived in the country and they had all sorts of fun together. Sometimes Baby Rook used to pick off tiny twigs and fir cones and drop them down from his home high up in the trees for Kitten to play with. Sometimes Puppy would roll his little rubber ball right down Rabbit's hole to play with. Sometimes Rabbit would pick a dandelion clock from the meadow and send the little white fluffets puffing up and up for Baby Rook to catch. Sometimes Kitten would hold her old cotton reel on a string in her sharp white teeth and let Puppy chase it round the garden. They were always thinking of new tricks to play and new things to do. And then, one day, when they had played their old games a hundred times and were sitting around thinking of something quite new to do, Kitten had a great idea.

'I know,' she cried. 'Let's all change houses for one night!'

'Change houses?' squawked Baby Rook.

'Change houses?' snuffled Rabbit.

'Change houses?' woofed Puppy.

They all cried together, 'What *do* you mean, Kitten?'

The small ginger kitten looked at them and she said, 'I mean, why shouldn't we all try living in one another's houses? Just for a change, of course, not for ever. I'm a good climber so I'd better go up in Rook's tree.'

'And I'm a good burrower,' said Puppy, 'so I could have a turn in Rabbit's home.'

'I couldn't bear to be shut up indoors,' said Baby Rook, 'so I'd better go in Puppy's box in the stable.'

'And that means I can sleep in Kitten's cosy basket by the fire,' said the little brown rabbit. 'What fun!'

As soon as they saw the sun was setting ready for bed the four little friends all thought they had better begin to settle into their new homes for the night.

Kitten looked up and down the high tree where Baby Rook's nest was tucked in between some twigs, and she wasn't so sure she wanted to sleep there after all. But she didn't like to say so because the others might think she was a cowardly cat. So she called 'Good night!', dug her sharp little claws into the rough bark of the tree, and began to climb.

Puppy looked down Rabbit's dark hole and he wasn't so sure he wanted to sleep there after all. But he didn't want the others to think he was afraid, so he called 'Good night!' and crept into the dark passage that went on and on and out of sight.

Baby Rook fluttered along to the stable where Puppy

slept in a box full of straw on the ground. It looked very low down and she thought it might be very dangerous if people should want to tread there. She wasn't so sure she wanted to sleep there after all. But all the others were going to their new homes and she wasn't going to be the only one left out, so she cawed 'Good night!' and hopped into the stable.

The little brown rabbit was left alone. He scuttled over to the back door and poked his head round. There inside, by the fire, was Kitten's basket with a soft cushion in it and a saucer of milk nearby. He didn't much like the idea of having no nice dark corner to huddle in, but he had nowhere else to sleep now, so in he went, plip-plop, plip-plop!

By the time Kitten had scrambled and clawed her way right up to Baby Rook's home, she was quite worn out. It felt very wobbly and chilly high up there in the

tree, but she was too tired to care any more and she curled round and tried to go to sleep.

By the time Puppy had scrambled and bumped his way along the dark stuffy passages to Rabbit's home, he was quite worn out. It felt damp and chilly under the ground, but he was too tired to care any more and he flopped down and tried to go to sleep.

By the time Baby Rook had poked and twisted the straw in Puppy's box into some sort of hollow to snuggle into, she was quite worn out. It felt dusty and hard in the box but she was too tired to care any more. She tucked her head down and tried to go to sleep.

By the time Rabbit had turned the cushion in Kitten's basket this way and that and poked his head underneath to shut out the light from the fire, he was quite worn out. It felt hot and stuffy in the kitchen and he kept hearing strange noises that upset him, but he was really too tired to care any more and he burrowed in as best he could and tried to go to sleep.

Presently the wind rose and the rain began to fall.

Baby Rook's nest swayed to and fro, high up in the tree. Kitten was very frightened. 'MIAOUGH! I'm not staying up here,' she said to herself and she began to hurry down to the ground again.

The rain grew heavier and heavier. Little cold streams of water trickled down Rabbit's passage and made puddles on the earth floor. Puppy was shivering and miserable. 'oo-ow!' he howled sadly. 'I'm not staying here any more.' And he hurried off down the passage to get above ground again.

The wind grew stronger and louder. The stable door creaked and squeaked and began to bang to and fro. Baby Rook was frightened.

'CAA-CAA!' she squawked. 'I'm not staying here. I might get shut in for ever.' And she flew out as fast as she could.

Inside by the fire it was warm enough and Rabbit didn't even know there was a storm blowing. But the fire crackled and spat and a cinder fell out near his fluffy coat. Rabbit was frightened. 'POOFF! I'm not staying here,' he said to himself. 'I might catch fire!' and he scuttled off as fast as he could go.

In a few minutes the storm was over and a big golden moon came shining out of the clouds. It shone down on the garden and the fields and what did it see? – One small ginger kitten, one small white puppy, one little brown rabbit, and one baby rook, all looking very lost and scared and all surprised to see each other. And it wasn't long, I can tell you, before Kitten was curled up cosily in her basket; Puppy was snuggled down in his box of straw; little brown Rabbit was safely underground in his burrow; and Baby Rook was swaying peacefully away high up in her tree-top.

And none of them ever suggested playing the 'All Change!' game again!

The Five Little Foxes
and the Tiger

ONCE upon a time, on the plains of East Pakistan, a fox and his wife lived in a snug little hole.

They had five children who were too young to feed themselves, and so every evening Mr and Mrs Fox crept out of their hole and made their way to the bazaar or market place, which was full of roughly-made stalls.

But they didn't go there to buy anything. They waited until all the people had gone home to their suppers, and then the two foxes crept among the stalls looking for scraps of food for their children.

Sometimes they found nothing but a few grains of rice or shreds of pumpkin but at other times they picked up quite large pieces of fish or meat which had been dropped unnoticed by a stall-holder.

Then the two foxes were overjoyed and would hurry home talking happily together.

But no matter who had found the most food – and to be truthful it was nearly always Mrs Fox who was the better scavenger – Mr Fox was so full of pride at his cleverness that he could not stop boasting.

'How much sense have you got, my dear?' he would ask his wife as they hurried along between large tufts of brown grass and withered-looking bushes.

'About as much as would fill a small vegetable basket,' Mrs Fox would reply modestly.

Then after a few minutes she would say, 'And how much sense have you got, my good husband?'

'As much as would fill twelve large sacks, needing twelve strong oxen to carry them,' the conceited Mr Fox would reply time and time again.

Now one evening, when the two foxes were on their way home with food for their children, and Mr Fox had just told his wife for the hundredth time how clever he was, a large tiger suddenly stepped out from behind a bush and barred their way.

'At last I've got you,' growled the tiger, showing them his sharp white teeth which glistened in the moonlight.

Mr Fox began to tremble and his legs gave way, so that he crumpled into a heap and lost the power to speak.

But clever Mrs Fox held her head high, and looking straight into the flashing eyes of the tiger, she said with a smile, 'How glad we are to have met you, O Uncle! My husband and I have been having an argument, and since neither will give way to the other, we decided that we would ask the first superior animal who crossed our path to settle the matter for us.'

The tiger was surprised at being spoken to so politely, and also flattered at being called 'Uncle', which is a term of great respect in Pakistan.

So he did not spring at the foxes to kill and eat them, but replied, 'Very well. I will help you if I can. Tell me what you were arguing about.'

'My husband and I have decided to part company,' said Mrs Fox in a clear, calm voice, while her husband, who had closed his eyes in fear, now opened them wide in surprise. 'But we have five children waiting at home for us, and we cannot decide how to divide them between us fairly. I think that I should have three, since I have had to spend more time in looking after them than my husband, and that he should have only two.

But my husband insists that I let him have the three boy-cubs, and that I keep only the two girl-cubs. Now, O wise Uncle, who do you think is right?'

When Mrs Fox saw the tiger licking his lips she knew that he was thinking that somehow he must have the five fox cubs as well as their parents for his dinner. And this was exactly what she had hoped for.

'I must see the cubs for myself before I can make a decision,' said the tiger. 'Will you take me to your home?'

'Certainly,' said Mrs Fox. 'We will lead the way, and you shall follow.'

The Five Little Foxes and the Tiger

Poor Mr Fox was completely at a loss to know what his wife was doing, but thinking that anything would be better than being eaten alive by a tiger, he staggered to his feet and followed his wife along the rough track, until they reached their home.

'Wait here,' said Mrs Fox to the tiger. 'You are too big to get inside our hole, so we will bring the children outside for you to see.'

She turned to her husband to tell him to go in, but he, needing no encouragement to get away from the tiger, shot into the opening like a flash.

Mrs Fox went in more slowly, talking all the time, saying that she would not keep him waiting more than a moment, and thanking him for being so gracious as to promise to judge their case for them.

Once inside their hole, the foxes gathered their children together as far away from the opening as possible, and in whispers told them what had happened.

'Don't make a sound,' said Mrs Fox, 'and presently the tiger will realize he has been tricked, and will go away.'

She was right. The tiger waited for hours, first patiently then furiously, as it gradually dawned on him that the foxes had no intention of letting him see their children, and when the sun rose the next morning, he had to go hungrily away.

After this, Mr and Mrs Fox went by a different path to the bazaar, and kept a sharp look-out for tigers.

Mr Fox never again asked his wife how much sense she had, but once or twice, when he showed signs of becoming proud again she would say to him, 'How much sense have you got, my dear?' and he would answer with an embarrassed laugh, 'Oh! About as much as would fill a small vegetable basket – a very small one, I'm afraid.'

Peter and the Rabbits

ONCE upon a time there was a farmer who had three sons: John, Jacob and Peter. And all three were un-believably lazy. They actually ate with only one eye open so the other eye could rest.

It so happened that one day John, who was the oldest, read in the newspaper that the king was looking for a keeper for his rabbits. Furthermore, anyone who could tend the rabbits for four days without losing even one of them would marry the princess and become king. This did not seem to be too much trouble, so John picked up his cap, put a few things in a sack and pre-pared to leave. His father suggested that he might not find the job quite so easy as he thought, but John was determined to go. He wanted to marry the princess and be king.

So he set off.

The way to the castle led through a large forest. And in the middle of the forest, John came upon an old woman. She was pulling and tugging and crying be-cause her nose was caught fast in the trunk of a tree. John laughed when he saw her.

'Don't be such a lout,' croaked the old woman, 'help me out of here. It's been over a hundred years since I came to cut down this tree and got caught. I'm starving. It's so long since I've eaten.'

John laughed even louder and said, 'Pull harder, old

woman, and your nose will be even longer.' Then he swung his sack over his shoulder and went on his way.

Finally he came to the king's castle. The king received him kindly and immediately made him chief rabbit keeper.

'But you must understand,' said the king, 'that if even one rabbit is lost, you will be thrown into the snake pit.'

With that, he let the rabbits out of their hutch, and

before John knew what had happened, they had all run off into the forest. John spent the whole day searching, but he found not so much as one rabbit. When evening came he had to admit that the rabbits were lost. It was into the snake pit with John.

When John did not come home, the second son, Jacob, was determined to follow his brother. Again the father gave good advice, but Jacob paid no attention. One morning, he too set off to see the king. Unfortunately, he was no better than his older brother. He also laughed at the old woman in the woods and made no move to free her.

At the king's castle he was received as kindly as his brother and made chief rabbit keeper at once. 'But you must understand,' said the king, 'that if even one rabbit is lost, you will be thrown into the snake pit.'

By the evening Jacob had lost all the rabbits. It was into the snake pit with Jacob.

The youngest son, Peter, waited at home for his brothers to return. But nothing happened. Of John and Jacob there was no word at all. Finally Peter packed his sack for a journey.

'Creampuffs and cheese!' he said to his father. 'The time has come for me to seek my fortune. Four days of rabbit keeping and I will marry the princess and be king.'

'I wish you good fortune,' said his father. 'But this rabbit keeping is more like rabbit trapping, I think. It's too clever for you. Why don't you stay home and herd the pigs, it's less dangerous.' But Peter could not bring himself to stay at home, and one day he was off.

On the way through the woods, he too came to the old woman.

She stood there as before, pulling and tugging at her nose.

'Good day, Mother,' said Peter, 'and what is the problem with your nose?'

'Ah, if only you'd help me,' the old woman said. 'A

hundred years I have stood here, and I cannot get my nose out of this tree. You can't imagine how hungry I am.'

Without a word, Peter took his axe, chopped down the tree, and freed the woman. Then he opened his sack and gave her something to eat. When she had finished, there was not much left for Peter. She had eaten everything he had.

'As a token of my thanks,' she said, 'I give you this flute. When you blow upon it, all the things you ask will come together; they will come together and remain together. They must come, and they must remain.'

'What a wonderful flute,' said Peter. 'And how useful.' He thanked the old woman and went on his way.

Finally Peter came to the castle; he went to the king, and the king made him chief rabbit keeper. 'But you must understand,' said the king, 'that if even one rabbit is lost, you will be thrown into the snake pit.'

'That seems fair,' said Peter, putting his hat on. The king opened the door of the rabbit hutch and, as always, the rabbits sprang out into the forest.

'Creampuffs and cheese, but they can run!' said Peter. Then he strolled leisurely into the woods, picked a few wild berries, and settled down in the cool shade of the trees. In the evening he took out his flute, blew a few notes on it, and from all sides the rabbits came running. 'Well, it's time to get on with it,' said Peter, and he set off with the rabbits for the castle.

As Peter came up to the castle, the royal family looked out of the window in amazement.

'Well,' said the astonished king, 'here is one who is better than most.'

'But not one to marry our daughter,' said the queen.

'No plum cake seems so very fine
No rabbit keeper will be mine,'

said the princess.

The king immediately held a meeting of his ministers, and they worked out a plan. The next day the princess was to disguise herself as a farm girl and go into the woods and buy a rabbit from Peter.

So on the second day, Peter and his rabbits were approached by a farm girl. But it was not a farm girl, and Peter knew it. Instead it was the princess.

'Good day,' said Peter, pretending he was speaking to a farm girl. 'And where might you be going?'

'Oh, do help me,' groaned the princess. 'I am in terrible trouble. If I don't bring a rabbit home with me tonight, I shall lose my head.'

'Creampuffs and cheese, now that's a pretty fix,' said Peter. 'Of course, I'll help you. But if I give you a rabbit, you must give me a kiss.'

'Well, you're a fresh one,' said the princess. 'But if that's what you ask that's what you must have, though never in my life have I kissed a man. Let me do it quickly while there is no one here to see us.' So she gave him a kiss, and he gave her a rabbit, which she quickly stuffed into a basket.

She walked contentedly to the edge of the woods, until Peter blew his flute. Then the rabbit sprang out of the basket and fled into the woods. And the princess went home unhappy.

'Where is the rabbit?' asked the king and queen, who were waiting impatiently for her at the castle.

'Oh,' she cried, 'I had a rabbit in my basket, bought at a great price, but it sprang out and ran into the woods.'

'Well,' scolded the queen, 'I could certainly have brought a rabbit home in a basket. In the morning I will go to the woods, and I will certainly bring back a rabbit.'

The next morning the queen disguised herself as a farm wife and set out to see Peter in the woods. Peter recognized her at once, but he didn't say so.

'Well, my good woman,' he said, what brings you to the middle of this big forest?'

'Oh, my dear young man,' said the queen, 'I am

looking for a rabbit. If I can't find one, I shall lose my head.'

'Why, how unpleasant,' said Peter. 'Fortunately, I can help you. I will give you a rabbit if you will stand on your head and waggle your feet in the air for me.'

'Never have I heard such insolence,' said the queen. 'But I suppose I must make the best of a bad bargain. And no one will know if I do it quickly while there is no one here to see.' So the queen stood on her head and waggled her feet, and Peter gave her a rabbit. She put it quickly into her coat, buttoned it up firmly, and hurried back towards the castle. But before she arrived, Peter blew his flute, and the rabbit whisked out of the jacket and back into the woods. So the queen, too, came to the castle without a rabbit.

The king was furious. 'Two stupid women!' he shouted. 'I don't think either of you really bought a rabbit. In the morning I will go to the woods, and you will see how such things should be done.'

On the fourth and last day, Peter saw a farmer and his donkey coming towards them. 'Creampuffs and cheese,' muttered Peter in surprise, 'it's the king himself. I must be careful not to let him see I know him.'

'Ho there, good man, do you go to market?' asked Peter in a loud voice.

'No, I wish I did. I wish I were anywhere but in this deep wood,' lamented the king. 'I am here to find a rabbit; and if I don't find one by tonight, it will cost me my life.'

'Ah, you have my sympathy,' said Peter. 'One rabbit more or less does not seem that important. So let me help you. You may have a rabbit if you will kiss your donkey's tail.'

'Well, you are a shameless one,' said the king. 'But what else can I do? I must have the rabbit. So let me do what I must while there is no one here to see me. I'll put this handkerchief on the tail and do as you ask.'

It was no sooner said than done, and the king received the rabbit. He grabbed it with both hands and ran as quickly as he could to the castle.

The queen and the princess were waiting for him on the castle steps. The trumpet sounded and out of the woods he came with his large farmer's hat pulled over his eyes. Peter hid behind a tree and watched as the king got off his donkey and strode eagerly towards the steps. At that moment the crafty boy blew on his flute. Up sprang the rabbit, out of the king's own hands, and ran off. The king looked very foolish, and the queen laughed, while the princess clapped her hands in pleasure.

'Where is the rabbit you were sure to bring?' they crowed.

The king grew fiery red and said, 'Just wait; we will see who laughs last.'

And the queen said, 'Of course, the boy will not have the princess.'

And the princess said:

> *No plum cake seems so very fine*
> *No rabbit keepers will be mine.*

Once more the king had a meeting with his ministers. So he was ready when Peter returned that evening with all the rabbits and demanded his reward: the king's crown and the princess for a wife.

'Slow, slow,' said the king. 'There is still something more you must do. You must first of all tell a whole sackful of truth. Only then can the marriage take place.'

Preparations began at once for the event. The carpenters built a huge stage. And then the tailor made an enormous sack. It took three days to get ready.

At the appointed time, Peter clattered up to the stage to the beat of drums and the sound of trumpets. Just below the stage sat the king, the queen and the princess. Behind them were large crowds of common people all making jokes and waiting to see how anyone could manage to tell a sackful of truth. When Peter began to speak, the chatter quieted.

'As you know,' he said in a sly voice, 'I must tell you a great deal of truth, in fact a whole sackful. So I will begin by reporting to you the strange things that happened to me as chief rabbit keeper. On the first day there was nothing odd that occurred. But on the second day there came a farm girl into the woods. Yet it was not really a farm girl, but your princess. She wanted a rabbit, and would pay any price. I gave it to her, but only after she had given me a kiss.'

The princess blushed red to both ears and wished she could sink into the ground. But the people thought it was the best story they had ever heard.

The queen whispered to the princess, 'You should have disguised yourself better. I'm sure I was not recognized.'

Meanwhile Peter continued to tell his sackful of

truth. 'On the third day an old farm wife came up to me. But not just any farm wife. This was your queen. She, too, wanted a rabbit. I agreed to give it to her, but only if she would stand on her head and waggle her feet.'

'The boor. The fresh thing!' cried the queen, who covered her face with a veil and said to the king, 'Let's not listen to any more of this. We've heard all we need to hear.' But the people shouted and clapped with pleasure.

The king himself laughed with all his might and said, 'You stupid women are all alike. There is, of course, no chance that he recognized me. Let's see what he says next.'

So Peter went on. 'On the fourth day an old farmer came riding by on his donkey. By now, I think you know who it was. You're right, it was the king himself. And like the others, he wanted a rabbit, cost what it might. I agreed to give him one, but first he had to –'

'Stop, stop,' shrilled the king, springing to his feet. 'The sack is full. The sack is full.'

At once Peter threw his hat in the air with joy and clattered down the steps from the stage. The people stamped and shouted.

Peter strode proudly over to the king and received his reward.

'A more intelligent son-in-law I could find nowhere in the world,' said the king. And he added in a loud voice, 'I am more than delighted to give you the princess.'

With the people watching and approving of all that

happened, Peter was dressed in kingly robes, the king himself placed the crown upon his head, and the princess took her place at his side. After seven days the wedding was held with great ceremony. The young queen came to love Peter very much, and so he lived happily and contented all his life long.

Acknowledgements

WE are most grateful to the undermentioned publishers and authors for permission to include the following stories:

Philippa Pearce for *Lion at School*.
Leila Berg for *The Lory who Longed for Honey* from *The Nightingale*.
E. P. Dutton & Co., Inc. for *How the Engine Learned the Knowing Song* from *Here and Now Story Book* by Lucy Sprague Mitchell. Copyright, 1921, by E. P. Dutton & Co., renewal copyright 1952 by Lucy Sprague Mitchell. Reprinted by permission of the publishers, E. P. Dutton & Co., Inc.
Messrs Blackie & Son Ltd for *The Five Little Foxes and The Tiger* and *One Little Pig and Ten Wolves* from *Animal Folk Tales Round the World* retold by Kathleen Arnott.
Longman Young Books for *Peter and the Rabbits* by Arthur Kübler. Used by permission of Atheneum Publishers. English translation by Roseanna Hoover. Copyright © 1969 by Artemis Verlag, Zurich, Switzerland. First U.S.A. edition 1969 by Atheneum Publishers, Inc. English translation copyright © 1969 by Atheneum Publishers, Inc.
Houghton Mifflin Company for *Jacoble Tells the Truth* by Lisl Weil.
William Collins Sons & Co. Ltd for *Pierre* by Maurice Sendak. Copyright © 1962 by Maurice Sendak. Reprinted by permission of Harper & Row Publishers.
Hodder & Stoughton Children's Books (formerly Brockhampton Press) Ltd for *The Two Giants* by Michael Foreman;

Acknowledgements

The Birds Concert by H. E. Todd; and *All Change!* by Ursula Hourihane.

Faber & Faber Ltd for *Tim Rabbit's Magic Cloak* from *Lavender Shoes: Eight Tales of Enchantment* by Alison Uttley.

J. M. Dent & Sons Ltd for *The Little Boy and His House* by Stephen Bone and Mary Adshead.

The Viking Press, Inc. for *The Little Rooster and the Diamond Button* from *The Good Master* by Kate Seredy. Copyright 1935, copyright © renewed 1963 by Kate Seredy. Reprinted by permission of the Viking Press, Inc.; and also George Harrap & Co. Ltd.

John Yeoman for *A Drink of Water*.

Alfred A. Knopf, Inc. for *Little Lisa* from *Tales from the North* by Einar Nerman. Copyright 1946 by Einar Nerman. Reprinted by permission of Alfred A. Knopf.

V. H. Drummond for *Little Laura and the Lovely Ostrich*.

We should also like to express our thanks for their willing and valuable help to Hazel Wilkinson, Lecturer, and Christine Jupp, former Children's Librarian, both of Wall Hall College of Education; to Mary Junor, Schools' Librarian, Barnet; to Mrs S. Stonebridge, Principal Children's Librarian, Royal Borough of Kensington and Chelsea; to Miss V. Newton, the Children's Librarian of the Chelsea Library; to Eileen Leach, Chief Librarian, Watford Junior Libraries; to Carole Francis, former Junior Librarian, Golders Green; and to Phyllis Hunt, Children's Editor at Faber & Faber, for constant advice and guidance.

More Young Puffins

THE GHOST AT NO. 13

Gyles Brandreth

Hamlet Brown's sister, Susan, is just too perfect. Everything she does is praised and Hamlet is in despair – until a ghost comes to stay for a holiday and helps him to find an exciting idea for his school project!

RADIO DETECTIVE

John Escott

A piece of amazing deduction by the Roundbay Radio Detective when Donald, the radio's young presenter, solves a mystery but finds out more than anyone expects.

RAGDOLLY ANNA'S CIRCUS

Jean Kenward

Made only from a morsel of this and a tatter of that, Ragdolly Anna is a very special doll and the six stories in this book, are all about her adventures.

SEE YOU AT THE MATCH

Margaret Joy

Six delightful stories about football. Whether spectator, player, winner or loser these short, easy stories for young readers are a must for all football fans.

THE RAILWAY CAT'S SECRET
Phyllis Arkle

Stories about Alfie, the Railway Cat, and his sworn enemy Hack the porter. Alfie tries to win over Hack by various means with often hilarious results.

WORD PARTY
Richard Edwards

A delightful collection of poems – lively, snappy and easy to read.

THE THREE AND MANY WISHES OF JASON REID
Hazel Hutchins

Jason is eleven and a very good thinker so when he is granted three wishes he is very wary indeed. After all, he knows the tangles that happen in fairy stories!

THE AIR-RAID SHELTER
Jeremy Strong

Adam and his sister Rachel find a perfect place for their secret camp in the grounds of a deserted house, until they are discovered by their sworn enemies and things go from bad to worse

MR MAJEIKA AND THE HAUNTED HOTEL

Humphrey Carpenter

Class Three of St Barty's are off on an outing to Hadrian's Wall with their teacher Mr Majeika (who also happens to be a magician).

Stranded in the fog when the tyres of their coach; are mysteriously punctured, they take refuge in a nearby hotel called The Green Banana. Soon some very spooky things start to happen. Strange lights, ghostly sounds and vanishing people . . .

NO PRIZE OR PRESENTS FOR SAM

Thelma Lambert

Sam just has to find a pet to enter in the Most Unusual Pets Competition at the village fete. But the animal he chooses leads to some very unexpected publicity! When Sam decides he'll give his Aunty and Uncle a happy Christmas, the only problem is how can he earn some money?

SUN AND RAIN

Ann Ruffell

It hasn't rained for seven weeks. The Smallwood family have had enough, and are sending off for all sorts of heat-wave 'special offers'. First to arrive is Susan's rain-making kit, and soon a rain cloud appears in the spotless blue sky – one solitary cloud which is fixed firmly over the Smallwoods' house!